Catastrophe

A Scottish Wildcat's

Tail

lucinda@dragonsdome.co.uk
http://www.dragonsdome.co.uk/
http://thedragonwhispererdiaries.blogspot.co.uk/

Published by Thistleburr Publishing

Catastrophe ~ A Scottish Wildcat's Tail

Thistleburr Publishing, ISBN: 978-0-9574718-4-9

Also by Lucinda Hare

The Dragonsdome Chronicles

The Dragon Whisperer
Flight to Dragon Isle
Dragon Lords Rising
The Stealth Dragon Services
Dark Dragon Dreams

The Fifth Dimension Chronicles

The Sorcerers Glen

Adult/Child Art Therapy Colouring / Conservation Books

Seadragon ~ Songs of the Sea
Falling for Autumn

Scottish Wildcat Conservation groups

'Often referred to as the Tiger of the Highlands, it is striking, handsome and powerful, the very essence of a wild predator living by stealth and strength. Sadly, Scottish wildcats are now one of our most endangered mammals and are on the edge of extinction.'

http://www.scottishwildcataction.org

Scottish Wildcat Action is the first national conservation plan with a vision to restore viable populations of Scottish wildcats north of the Highland fault line. The partnership includes: The Scottish Government, Scottish Natural Heritage, Scottish Wildlife Trust, Royal Zoological Society for Scotland, Forestry Commission Scotland, Cairngorms National Park Authority, National Museums Scotland, National Trust for Scotland, Royal (Dick) Veterinary School, University of Edinburgh, Scottish Land & Estates, Scottish Gamekeepers Association and many more.

http://www.wildcathaven.co.uk/
http://www.scottishwildcats.co.uk/
http://treesforlife.org.uk/forest/missing-species-rewilding/the-scottish-wildcat/
http://www.scottishwildcats.co.uk/conservation.html
http://cairngorms.co.uk/look-after/conservation-projects/cairngorms-wildcat-project
http://www.nms.ac.uk/explore/collections-stories/natural-sciences/scottish-wildcat/

Faux fur sporrans

http://www.thescotlandkiltcompany.co.uk/synthetic-fur
http://www.vegetariansporran.com/dress-sporrans.html
http://www.proudlyscottish.com/acatalog/Scottish_Sporrans.html

In memory of beloved blind Smudge

Autumn ~ Harvest Moon

I woke to a cool dawn, my coat laden with dew and the taste of blood and bones still fresh in my mouth. It was a good hunt. High above, trapped by the grasping branches of a rowan tree, the corpulent moon turned everything to milk and moon-shadow. A tawny owl hooted softly to his mate as I rose and stretched my limbs, testing the layers of darkness with eyes and ears and nose. Leaf-litter and cool earth oozed between my pads. Soft sounds vibrated like plucked strings in the still air, shivering along the hairs of my pelt, describing this moonlit world for me in golden detail. Scents hugged the misty floor of the forest. I tasted them with my tongue, some fresh, some days old. Tracks criss-crossed the clearing; I read them as easily as any child's book. An old brock had passed me by in the early hours of the night. His sett lay to the north, beneath a chestnut tree brought down by early autumn winds. A dog fox and his vixen had stolen some time to play in the bracken before hunting for rabbit. Pellets of bone, sinew and skin are all that mark the passage of countless unwary mice and voles foraging for brambles beneath the golden harvest moon and the sharp eyes of the owls.

Wind fluted through bare branches with a feline hiss. The promise of dawn was a finger of light on the distant horizon and the feathered folk slept on; feathers fluffed against the cold, they felt safe at the end of their slender branches. Beneath them water leapt down its course, tumbling stones and silver trout into the loch. Dancing between silver birch and rowan, I paused to drink the freezing milky-blue snowmelt. Unsheathing my claws, I honed them on the deep-scored bark of an old witch-elder. Intruders beware!

The brittle leaves barely betrayed my thistledown passage. Like the year, they were old and dying; the sap that was their lifeblood drawn back into the tree that birthed them. Abandoned to the frosts, they lay in deep drifts, burying the hedgehogs and wood-mice beneath gossiping carpets of yellow and red leaves.

There was growing light at last as I floated across the dark, newly furrowed fields. A foolish cockerel took a deep breath and fell with a strangled squawk, his life ebbing faster than the night. As light blossomed in the east, I faded back into the fringe of the forest with my prize.

Hallowe'en

The moon waxed and waned. Winter drew closer and the sun grew ever lazier.

Wrapped in a jacket of yellow fog she could scarcely be bothered to rise. Perhaps she was like the hedgehog, and would hibernate all winter beneath a blanket of fog and frost? The mighty chestnut trees shed their prickly bounty, shaken by storms that drove the sheep with their woolly coats behind the feeble shelter of dry-stane pens. Children invaded the woodlands, weary parents in tow; they stamped with glee on the green armoured shells, releasing the russet and white kernels snuggled at their hearts. Threading them with string they fought, squealing loudly, crying out when their careless fingers were caught.

The wind swung to the east, bringing with it the promise of snow and a hard winter. The pheasants quarrelled and quibbled in stubble fields, fighting for drops of grain. They were easy to catch, being slow and stupid. Musical geese flew high overhead, heading for warmer climes, their white wings touched to gold as the sun went down. Dusk was netted by filigree cobwebs pearled with dew, each drop ruby red. Night threw down his mantle; the moon had yet to rise.

The owl hooted.

The fox barked.

The hunt was on again.

The Furless-Ones

Early snow lay crisp on the ground when I heard them shout to each other out on the moors where the grouse nest. In the woods I could hear them stumbling around, clattering from tree to tree, loud as magpies. Everything fled before them. A chocolate-brown pine marten hid in a hollow tree. A red squirrel took graceful flight through the air.

From the safety of the forest I had watched these furless two-legs since I was a litter-cub. They are strange animals indeed who walk upright on their hind legs and have no tail or feathers to help them balance. Pale, and soft skinned as the underbelly of a slug, the furless-ones steal the pelts and coats of others to survive. Yet there are colours and shapes their eyes do not see. There are sounds they cannot hear. Their noses are too far from the ground and are surely useless for tracking. For furless-ones the landscape is forever fixed. To me, every subtle shade, every scent on the wind, every track tells a story. But the furless-ones have fire, and they have guns, and like all furred and feathered creatures of woods and moors, I greatly feared them.

Bang! Sound splintered through the forest. My paws burst into a run before my ears and eyes could identify the danger. A red fox bounded over bracken and bramble. Dogs barked.

Bang, bang! Instinct led me blindly racing through the trees towards my winter den, a cairn of rocks at the fringe of the forest where it opens

3

onto moorland. Thump…thump…thump…thump…my heart slammed against my chest.

Fleeing pheasants ran this way and that, colliding with each other in their panic. A capercaillie cowered down. Rabbits hurtled into the dark safety of their burrows. I had no time for them now. Briars tore and whipped. A freezing burn; a fleeting flash of foam and silver beneath my paws. Two red deer leapt past me. A pheasant finally took to the air, its feathers whirring.

Bang! Its broken body thudded to the ground, spilling its red-jewelled feathers all over me. I panicked. Thump, thump… thump, thump… Now I was leaping frantically from boulder to rock to fallen tree… closer… closer, not far to go. Thump, thump…

Bang! My hindquarters exploded in hot bright pain and I was flung sideways into a rock. Falling… falling… I tumbled to the ground. Leaves drifted down gold on blood red to cover me. I drifted with them…down and down…

The Car

I lifted my hammering head. The rest of my body was twisted and wooden as the roots that dug into my flank. The evening was dark and cold, but inside I was on fire. Bone scraped on bone. I tried to clean and tend my wounds but the effort was too much. When I woke the second time, the moon had crested the trees, and cold white stars were embedded in the indifferent blanket of night. I could barely feel anything but grinding pain as I dragged myself across a clearing. I had no idea of where I was going. I was driven only by the animal instinct to hide. Somewhere… anywhere…

The forest suddenly dipped down onto a dirt track road. I tumbled down like a breath of wind, surprised at how the cold Earth hugged my heavy body to her. Leaf litter settled, along with the first flakes of snow. I lay there as my blood turned cold and night's frosty fingers ate into me.

A distant roar carried through the woods. A large creature bounced along the track, the glow from its two eyes torching the woodland to sudden colour. I had seen such a fearsome thing before but only from a great distance. Its voice sounded like a hundred tawny owls screeching.

Closer and closer it came, and still I could not move, my blooded fur froze me to the ground. The creature squealed. A blast of hot rank breath rolled over me then sudden silence fell. Doors banged. I managed to open one swollen eye. Yellow light curled round two shadows. Two-legs! Humans! The furless-ones! I tried to flee but my thoughts remained my own; my body didn't hear them. Boots crunched on stone. Shadows loomed out of the night. There was a sudden intake of breath; its owner's voice tight with concern as she knelt beside me.

'Oh, George! Look! Look at all that blood. George, we must get him to a vet. He must have been hit by a car!' She reached out to brush my fur. 'He's frozen. He's barely alive.' I spat blood and tried to strike, but my paw barely twitched. I was as helpless as a kitten.

His deep voice was surprisingly gentle. 'He's a wildcat, Mary. Look at those eyes, that thick, bushy, black-tipped tail. Best put him out of his misery.' He peered closer and sucked in his breath. 'Looks like he's been shot.' A torch was held closer, warm fingers probing gently.

'Yes, look, there and there. Pellets! Some gamekeeper's shot him. I'll get the spade from the boot.'

'George, no!' Mary's voice cracked. 'He's still alive; he's still in with a fighting chance. We must at least try. Here…' She took off her coat. I remember it was the colour of rowanberries in the warm yellow light. 'Wrap him in this.'

'He might not survive the journey, Mary,' her husband warned. 'We've a long way to go yet.'

'I know...'

'Sorry, old chap, but this is going to hurt.' George grunted as he tried to lift me.

'Good grief, but he's huge, Mary!'

Night's frozen fingers were loath to give up their bounty. Fur tore. Hot blood spilled. I didn't think I had any left in me. Pain exploded in a sickening surge, with fear hard on its heels. I mewled, and then the dark night wrapped me in its dreamless mantle.

The Veterinary Hospital

I remember little of that long journey save the noise, and the endless jolt and bump of the car on the road. I drifted on the edge of death. More movement. Bright lights. Strange, harsh smells.

'Yes, he's a wildcat all right,' a brisk thoughtful voice. 'A youngster, probably not more than a year old. He's in superb condition. That's probably what's kept him alive.'

'We think he's been shot.'

Gentle, knowing hands examined me.

'No question. A twelve-bore shotgun. See the lead pellets? Two broken legs, multiple fractures. Looks like a gamekeeper's had a go at him. There are so few left in the wild,' he shook his head sadly. 'We'll admit him immediately into intensive care; give him painkillers, treat him for shock - '

'What does -?'

'He'll get a cage with a heated pad, intravenous fluids to counter dehydration and blood loss. Antibiotics to prevent infection. Once he's stabilised we'll take some x-rays to assess the extent of the damage, then surgery. I'll just give him an injection for the pain...'

'Then he'll survive?' Hope tinged her question.

The vet pursed his lips. 'I can't promise anything at this stage. It depends on so many factors. Provided there is no internal bleeding… Broken bones are not life-threatening in themselves but only certain fractures can be stabilised with a plaster cast. More commonly, surgery involving pinning and plates would be used. These injuries, particularly to this right hind leg may involve nerve damage, and if this is severe and permanent…' the vet paused. 'Then amputation of the limb is a distinct possibility. Same if the bone is too fragmented. He's going to be here quite a while.' There was a pause. 'It is going to be expensive…obviously, he's not insured…'

'How much?' You could hear her voice strung tighter than a cob's web.

'Hard to say, but hundreds…maybe a thousand.'

There was a soft indrawn breath. 'We'll find the money, somehow.' Mary's voice seemed suddenly small.

'Right. The nurse will give you a consent form to sign, and she'll take your phone number. I suggest you ring in four or five hours' time. We should have a clearer picture by then.'

A bee sting in the flank then I was floating like thistledown through the trees.

Thistledown Turned to Stone

I dare say the sun rose and fell but I never saw it. The days passed in a blur, one running into the other with little to distinguish them. It was a time of muddled memories where bright hard edges and sharp angles replaced the familiar leaf and stone and tree of home. Bandaged and drip-fed, I was netted in a dim twilight world, as helpless and fearful as any insect. If my eyes saw, then my brain forgot as I fought infection and injury.

All I knew for certain was that I didn't feel the wind's breath in my fur or the frosty grass beneath my paws as midwinter crept closer. I never heard the deer bark or the dog fox call as winter gave way to a snow-laden new year. I did not know it, but the fingernail moon grew fat and waned twice before I was to see the open sky again.

Then one morning, when crisp daylight streamed through the open window, I staggered awkwardly to my feet and found the cobwebs had blown away. A hand cradled my head. A woman slept, head awkwardly angled against the cage, long dark hair spilling over the blanket, her stiff fingers curled inwards like a dead spider. I drank in the scent of rowanberries that had drifted through my dreams. I slept again.

When I next woke, Mary was still there, sitting on the stool gazing at me. She made no move to open the cage, but a smile of soft encouragement lit up her pale face, with its dark flashing eyes that were not exactly night-black but not precisely earth-brown.

'You're awake, puss!' her voice was as gentle as wind through the barley.

Thirst burned my throat and swollen dry tongue. Watching her all the while, I drank and drank from the water dish. Then I slept. When I woke she had gone, but the next morning she was back again. And so as the long dreary days passed I came to watch for her, the only softness in this stark, sterile world.

The Car Again

'He's well enough to be taken home?'

The vet nodded. 'You do realise that wild cats are not like ordinary cats?'

Mary nodded anxiously, her eyes swivelling to mine. 'I've been reading up on the Web. There are hardly any left in the wild; some say less than forty! He has to survive!'

'Hhmmn.' The vet was dubious. 'Do you have any pets?' she asked finally, brushing hair from her eyes.

'Yes…Haggis.'

8

'Haggis?'

'She's a grumpy old lady of about sixteen.'

'Ah,' she warned. 'Well, you'll have to be careful. Wildcats are much stronger and have faster reactions than your average domestic moggie. They can't be domesticated. He will be very destructive; at best he's going to be a right handful. If you've got any new furniture that you want to keep that way, don't let him in the same room. Now… food. A diet of only tinned cat food and biscuits won't go down very well.'

'What should I…?'

'Rabbit and pheasant ~ that's what we've been giving him. I mean they eat everything from grouse to hare, frogs, fish, squirrels and birds…collecting road kill might be a good idea. That's what we've tried and it worked a treat.'

'Right…' but Mary pulled a face and sounded far from convinced.

'Problems?'

'No…not really. It's just that I'm vegetarian.'

The vet found this amusing. 'Well, you'll have to forget about being squeamish if you intend looking after this chap.'

They looked into my cage. I drew back into the shadow and hissed. There was nowhere to fly to, and anyway I was still so weak that I could barely stand. A man walked into the room, laughter curling the edge of his lips. He was tall and broad shouldered, with the face and eyes of a hawk.

'Oh, George,' Mary turned her face up towards his. 'He's ready to come home. Aren't you, puss?'

'He's wild, darling,' her husband cautioned. 'You can't tame him. Once he's well, he'll be off. Don't get too attached.'

'But George,' tears sprang and spilled. 'The vet says his back leg may never properly mend. He might not be able to survive in the wild.'

'Have you far to travel?' The vet had brought in a light cage and placed it on the surgery table.

'About an hour,' Mary answered, as she gave the keys to her husband. 'The car's parked just outside the door.'

The car!

Cars have coloured and armoured carapaces like beetles do; only cars are as hollow inside as a cave or a rotten oak. They have four strange legs rounded like the full moon and they growl and complain all the time. They can outrun the red deer following dark trails that criss-cross the moors and woods. At night their eyes gleam like ours in the dark, only the car's eyes are as fierce and blinding as the sun. And it eats furless-ones and their four-legged creatures but then spits them out unharmed or leaves them dead on the road. Oh, yes, I was afraid of this armoured beast.

'Let me.' Smiling encouragingly at me, George stepped forward and flicked open the catch. He reached into the cage.

The vet was pulling on gauntlets. She stepped forwards hastily from the door.

'I don't think that's a very good idea, Mr Dunsmore. He's very difficult to handle. Let m - '

But George had opened the cage and reached in.

'Argghhh!'

'Nurse, nurse!'

'Mary...how about you-try-and-get that front paw, ow! under control?'

'Got him! Argghhh!'

'He's huge!'

'He's got me!'

'Ow! Nearly got him. Just have to get a grip – no, really, it's only a small bite! I've had my tetanus shot.'

'Mary, prise that claw out of the table top, will you?'

'Mind that plaster cast!'

It took three of them in the end to wrap me in a blanket.

'I think,' the vet offered, as George ruefully sucked his bleeding fingers, 'that it might be better if he were sedated for the journey. Nothing strong, just a mild sedative to help you get him home. And we'll put this buster collar on. We can't have him worrying at the wounds.

They'll get itchy as they mend, so be prepared for that. Then let me tend to those bites, Mr Dunsmore.'

The familiar bee sting. I hissed. My legs wobbled, and paws and claws refused to obey. I sagged onto the blanket. My mind followed.

In due course, bandaged, sedated and collared, I was re-wrapped in a blanket and boxed up. I remember nothing except dark and warmth, the hard edge of the plastic collar and the rhythmic rattle and roll of the car bouncing along pot-holed tracks.

I think I slept, because next time I opened my eyes it was to something quite different.

Thistleburr Cottage

A small yellow lamp held the coming night at bay.

The study was a low-ceilinged room with bunches of drying herbs and berries hanging down from soot-blackened rafters. The lower part of the wall was panelled with warm dark wood and the upper part whitewashed with framed photographs of all sizes, hung higgledy-piggledy everywhere, and an old map above the mantelpiece.

Two deep-set windows were hidden behind armfuls of ivy and red berries. Old leather chairs plumped with bright patched cushions filled the room with curves and soft colours. Rugs and books lay scattered over the floor. An elderly grey tabby cat considered me with serene green eyes from one of the chairs. The stove beside my bed threw out drowsy warmth, and the familiar resinous smell of pinewood calmed me. I drank some water then slept. Even the door softly opening did not disturb my dreams.

'How's he doing, sweetheart?'

'He's drunk some water but taken no food. He's sleeping.'

'That's the best thing for him. Come to bed, Mary.'

'I'll just stoke the stove first.'

They tiptoed out.

The sun was long up when I next opened my eyes. Fresh air blew in an open window, bearing the sharp smell of snow. For a while I contented myself watching the play of dappled sunlight on the walls, and listening to sounds I had not heard in a long, long time: the cackle and chuckle of geese, the wind sighing through trees, the call of robin and blackbird. And beneath them all, the tumbling gurgle of a nearby burn. I could smell fresh turned earth in a dirt tray positioned behind a large pot plant, so wobbled my way out my bed to have a poke around. Reasonably satisfied, I made my way awkwardly back onto the bedding.

'Hello, puss. How are you feeling?'

I had grown so used to her scent that I had not noticed her sitting there at the small desk beneath one of the windows. I shrank from the sudden sound as far as the wood stove would allow. The plastic collar jammed so that I could barely move my head. I panicked, scrabbling frantically to free myself.

'Oh, puss,' she started from her chair. That set me to renewed frenzy. Finally free of the stove's grip, I searched for a way out to fresh air and freedom. I could barely stand as two paws went their own way, irrespective of where the other two might like to go. Heart racing, I careened around the room bumping into one thing then the next, the dull thumps driving me to new desperation to rid myself of this wretched thing round my neck. My weak legs wobbled and then gave up entirely. I collapsed in an untidy heap.

'Oh, puss,' Mary looked as shocked as I felt, as I lay there with my mouth wide open, lips drawn back panting furiously. 'Don't be afraid. I'm not going to hurt you. You've just got to mend, get your strength back. I'll give you plenty of time.'

The grey cat on her lap jumped down.

'Haggis, careful, old lady. Haggis!'

Ignoring her, the bony creature stalked across to me. I had no energy left to hiss let alone strike, but I had a go. Unoffended, she glided slowly forwards till her black nose nearly touched my pink one and her not exactly green and not quite yellow eyes met my not exactly yellow and not precisely green ones. Then her small pink tongue darted out, and she started to clean the fur around bandaged and plastered legs as if I were a litter-cub wet behind the ears!

Before I knew it, Haggis had moved in to share my bed!

Pilchards

'How about some pilchards? No, not you, Haggis, you greedy old thing. You've already had more than enough!' Mary gently lifted the elderly cat from her lap onto the floor.

Pilchards?

Ever so slowly, as was her habit, Mary moved towards me with a dish before placing it quietly on the floor in the middle of the room. Stretching fingertips, she pushed it towards me then slowly retreated back to her seat, never taking her eyes from me once.

'There you go, puss. You've got to eat more; you're still all skin and bone.'

Ignoring Mary's instructions, Haggis came over to help herself anyway. My tummy growled louder than I did, but I still waited respectfully till the old bag of bones had finished, before devouring the remains. I then suffered her attentive grooming. After all, I was in no position to clean myself, was I? Then I curled up as close as that hated collar would allow and slept. When I woke, Haggis was snoring loudly beside me and Mary was hunched over the desk, writing by lamplight. As if attuned to my tiniest of movements she turned her head towards me and smiled.

'I'm an author, puss. Well...' she looked at me with fierce determination. 'I *will* be some day! Just you see. They say you've just got to keep on trying. So I'm going to write a book about you.' She pointed to a pile of books and sheets of paper. 'I'm doing lots of research on the Web about wildcats so that I can understand you. Learn what makes you tick. And hopefully, puss,' she sighed, 'you'll learn to love me as much as I love you. To love the three of us.'

The third member of 'us' entered, as if on cue.

'Here, sweetheart,' the tall, dark-haired man put down a roll of old carpet along with some tools. 'Old Mrs Crombie had some off-cuts in her loft, just as you thought. Right, puss,' he looked at me with keen hazel eyes and smiled ruefully. 'Time to protect what's left of our furniture, don't you think? That front paw of yours is obviously mending fast; a little too fast!'

George set about examining the furniture. He sucked in his breath. 'I didn't realise he'd done quite so much damage!'

'It doesn't matter too much, though, does it?' Mary asked, anxiously moving down to kneel beside her husband. 'I mean, it was pretty old and battered when we bought it. A few more scratches here and there...?'

She trailed off as he pointed to the huge gouges on the table legs.

'Oopps...well it's a good sign in one way,' she said brightly. 'At least we know he's on the mend.'

George had to smile at that. 'Trust you to find something positive in everything.'

He hugged her to his side. 'Well, it's not as if we weren't warned. Serves me right for not getting round to it sooner.'

Haggis and I watched as he cut and stapled squares of old carpet around the bottom half of the leather chairs and the table legs.

'Right, puss,' he said with a grin. 'Scratch away as much as you like!'

It became a daily routine and then a familiar pattern, as hours turned to days and days to weeks. Mary would sit in a high-backed chair, head down over her laptop, quietly tapping away, or she would gaze into the distance in quiet contemplation, as if seeing a landscape that wasn't there, or she would pick up a book and quietly hum as she turned its whispering pages. And there were plenty to choose from. The entire room was given over to books of every shape, size and description. Little and large, old and new, thin and fat, they occupied every neuk and cranny, every shelf and every available surface. They were even stacked in precarious piles on the floor, growing ever upwards like stalagmites.

Weak as a kitten, I often wobbled and fell as I learnt to walk again. To begin with I was as clumsy as a goose on a frozen loch, and my damaged hind-leg ached. But alternately nudged and provoked by Haggis, I explored first the study and then the other rooms in the tiny cottage. I lost count of the times I fell trying to climb, bringing books and tablecloth tumbling to the floor with me. Mary and George tidied the mess up without a word of reproach. Then Mary fashioned steps out of books and boxes so that I could hobble up to join Haggis. We sat for endless hours gazing out from the windowsill at the world outside. I began to heal. But how I hated that plastic that collared me neatly as a foxglove bell, and how I longed to tear at the stitches that tightened and tormented and itched as my wounds healed.

George, Mary and Haggis lived deep in the rolling Perthshire hills. Most folk worked on surrounding farms, except for George. He was a Lecturer in maritime archaeology at Stirling University. Putting on his helmet and an assortment of leather jacket and waterproofs, he chugged off to work each day on an old motorbike, with armfuls of students' coursework packed into two battered and patched old saddlebags. The first time he brought a dead partridge in from the road, I dragged it into a corner, tearing mouthfuls of feathers so that I could crack the bones and release the sweet juices inside. Food never tasted so good!

Then one day in early spring we went back to the vet's. Haggis came with us. 'To keep you calm, puss, and stop you being frightened,' Mary said. Haggis seemed untroubled by the short trip and wrapped herself comfortingly around me till the rapid thumping of my heart quietened.

Deftly wrapping me in a towel with heavy leather gloves before I had time to react, the vet peeled off the stale dressings. 'He's mending well, but this hind leg will never be quite right. You see the x-ray here? These metal pins have knit well but there was just too much damage. That means this hind leg is always going to be stiff and it will get worse as he grows older, I'm afraid. But the front paw should be right as rain. We'll just take the cast off and replace the dressings on his hind leg. Do we need to sedate him?'

I was so grateful to be rid of it that I allowed the vet to remove the hot and itchy cast without biting her once.

'He's mellowing there, Mrs Dunsmore,' the vet smiled. 'I think you just might be making progress. He's young. He's adapting. I'll show you how to change the dressings yourself and in another few weeks or so, I think you can take the collar off.'

A Vole a Day Keeps the Vet at Bay

Mary was patient, oh so patient, and in the end that kindness wore down my defences.

Often she would sit on the floor reading a book, Haggis on her lap. Haggis would stretch from time to time and come over to wash me. Then she would stalk back to Mary and purr and insinuate herself outrageously for a tickle under the chin or a stroke on the tummy, lying with all four legs stuck in the air. A cat's natural curiosity made me

16

wonder what that was like, so that sometimes, unseen, I would rush in and have a quick sniff of Mary's jumper or shoe or hand. She never tried to corner me and I never tried to bite her. Then one evening Mary stretched out a hand to offer me a vole Haggis had caught and donated to the household pot.

'Here, puss.'

I graciously accepted the titbit and a bond sprang up between us. For the first time since I was a litter-cub I had a family. After that, Haggis frequently shared her kills. The March moon fattened and so did I.

Outside, as the days grew longer and warmer, the hillsides sprang to purple. The birch and alder and chestnut gathered legions of foxglove and bluebells about their feet. Bees gathered pollen and the swallows called as they swooped wildly on the wing. The lower pastures were loud with the bleat of lambs and the forest with the calls of capercaillie and fox. But as the lambs grew, so did my yearning for the hunt. As the moon waned and the days became longer, I started to sicken for the wild open spaces.

Old Jock

'Aye,' old Jock shook his head as he scratched me under the chin. 'He's a bonny beast, an' no mistake. All shades of smoke and sand and eyes like Cairngorm stones. Five rings on that magnificent thick tail. Don't see them very often these days; pure bred wildcats like this boy, that is. Now when I was a lad...'

Mary settled down by the hearth. I allowed her to lift me to her lap, from which vantage I could look down on the old man's dog; a small spindly affair; white and tan and with hardly any tail. It grinned and wagged what it did have. So, not all dogs are bad.

'... Aye, in the old days the keepers used to kill 'em on sight. Thought they were a threat to stocks of grouse. But then the Great War came along and the ghillies and keepers all went to die in the muddy fields of France. So few returned home...'

His thoughts drifted like mist. Mary waited in silence, respecting the moment.

'But with them all gone, yon cat spread as far south as Edinburgh and Glasgow. Aye, and now they're protected, but there are very few still in the wild. Yon keeper that shot him broke the law. They're beautiful beasties, and bring wealth to the north, what with the tourists who can stalk them now for photographs, not trophies.'

'So...it might happen again?' Mary was horrified. 'I never thought of that.'

'Dinnae fash yerself, lassie,' Old Jock said kindly. 'I can put the word out that this here laddie's a friend o' yours. He'll nae be harmed around here. Not by one o' us. We'll protect him.'

He scratched his head, tipping up his tweed cap, considering me. 'Now, here's a thought. Why don't you build him a pen?'

'A pen?'

'Aye, lass,' Old Jock nodded, now that the thought had taken hold of him. 'No' a wee dinky thing the size o' a rabbit hutch. A big pen like in yon Highland Wildlife Park. You've a fair bit of land with this here croft that's mostly going to waste forbye yon vegetable patch. Build a pen onto the back o' the house. He'll need to feel the wild open spaces, else he'll pine away and die.'

So they did.

The Wild Outdoors

'Right, puss,' Mary smiled, as she carefully scooped me from the sill and took me through to the kitchen, 'we've built a run for you outside and we've put in a bigger cat flap. In fact the largest we could find,' she pulled a face. 'I hope you can squeeze through! Look, we've taped it open to start with till you get the hang of it. The run isn't very large, but it has a cairn of boulders and an old tree stump for you to...'

I danced for the sheer joy of it. Clumsy or not, the chilly grass beneath my pads had never felt so good and the heady scent of heather made me dizzy, so that I reeled from bark to boulder. I sharpened my claws and drank in the cold fresh air that flowed down from the hills bringing a hundred scents with it. High above, a buzzard keened, but at that very moment I was freer than he was.

Letter from Aunt Edith

The only cloud on the horizon in this beautiful late spring was Mary's Aunt Edith. I'd barely had my stitches out when the letter dropped through the letterbox and onto the mat. Spidery handwriting crawled across it with a wobbly hand. Mary opened it eagerly. She read it twice, which made her twice as miserable.

'Oh, puss!' She put her arms around me and had a little cry. By the time her husband arrived home from work she was ready for another.

'Darling?' He knelt beside us. 'Is that another letter from Aunt Edith?'

His wife nodded handing it to him.

'Her condition is getting worse?'

She nodded. 'She's... oh, George! I think she's losing her mind. She talks about thieves and hidden treasure. Most of it makes no sense. She's asking why we haven't visited! Why we weren't up at the castle for Christmas!'

'But...' George frowned. 'But your Aunt Maud specifically said her sister didn't want any visitors at Christmas, because she was too poorly! And you must have rung twice every week since to check on her progress.'

'I know! That's why it doesn't make any sense. Read it.'

He scanned the rest of the letter's contents.

'I see what you mean, darling, but she's not a well old lady. Not well at all...' He paused. 'Listen, let's go up and see her this weekend. We haven't seen her since our honeymoon. My teaching will be finished by eleven tomorrow and I've none on Monday. Let's make it a long weekend.'

Mary's face lit up, but then a thought struck her. 'But how about puss?'

George looked at me. 'I think he can cope without us for a few days. He'll have Haggis for company and you could ask Susie from next door to look in to set the fire and feed them. What do you say?'

Mary smiled. 'I'll ring to say we're coming,' but her hand hesitated over the phone.

'Aunt Maud?'

Mary grimaced as if she'd just eaten a sour plum. 'Aunt Maud.' she agreed.

'She intimidates me quite deliberately, and she always says it's for Aunt Edith's own good, that her sister is far too poorly to receive visitors, or to answer my letters. When I try and insist, she twists my words around and says I'm just being selfish and thinking only of myself.'

'I'll ring,' George said firmly, taking the phone from his wife's hand. 'And I'll not let that old baggage bully me. I'll tell her we're coming whether she likes it or not. I'll not let her say no!'

And he didn't.

It was the first of many weekend partings as Mary's Aunt's condition slowly improved. And I, fierce wildcat that I am, I missed Mary. Well, not her, you understand, but all the little creature comforts that she provided. And only because, let me make it quite clear, only because I was still an invalid.

The Call of the Wild

The weather turned mild. The midges were back, hovering in great clouds over the burn. Birds were building nests and pigeons were courting, when I first picked up her scent on the wind that blew down from the hills. Over the following days she came closer and closer until I saw her watching me through the long grass. She was quite small with burning gold eyes and a long soft creamy pelt of banded smoke. It was love at first sight. Cats are not made for digging, but rabbits had already undermined the pen. The three-quarter moon was on the rise when I heard her call. Slipping under the netting, I went to her.

The hunt was on.

The moon rose and fell twice while we hunted hare and rabbit and other small game that ranged across her territory. By then she was heavy with kitten and had chosen her den to rear them, an old badger sett in the woods. As the swallows dipped and dived for insects, she gave birth to a litter of seven kittens.

I brought food to the den over the next three moons. By then the kittens were weaned and we taught them how to hunt. As the harvest ripened yellow in the fields, and the kittens' eyes turned from ice-blue to saffron-gold, we parted our many ways and my thoughts turned back towards a whitewashed cottage, a dark-haired woman, and a bony grey cat with serene green eyes called Haggis.

The Wanderer Returns

The harvest moon peeked over the heather-clad Perthshire hills. The valley below lay serenely in shades of blue and black. A light wind whispered through the trees, bringing with it familiar scents of wood smoke, people and cooking, from the cottages down by the burn. Windows and doors spilled dandelion yellow into the night. I threaded through the long grass and poppies towards home. The field was alive with vole and mice and rabbit, grown fat and lazy in my absence. Plenty time for them to learn that I had returned.

A shade of night detached itself from beneath the old chestnut. Haggis greeted me affectionately with little chirrups of pleasure and immediately started grooming me as if I had only been out for an evening stroll. A dish of milk and cat food had been left outside the backdoor, a ritual that looked as if it had occurred every night since I had left, given the size of the hedgehog who was greedily slurping the last drops from the plate. My nose led me instead to the kitchen table, where a stew was cooling on the hob. It was extremely good and I ate too much, and then fell asleep curled beside the range. I awoke to the sounds of Haggis getting a serious telling off. I cautiously poked my head around the kitchen door.

Eyes that were not exactly night-black but not precisely earth-brown met my not exactly yellow and not precisely green ones. Mary opened her mouth but nothing came out. The stew pan fell unnoticed from lifeless fingers. She didn't even blink when it clattered messily to the floor. Not one to miss an opportunity, Haggis dived in.

'Sweetheart,' George's voice called unheeded from the bedroom. 'Is everything OK?'

Then Mary threw herself at me, holding me close as if I might vanish like the morning mist, making incoherent little chirrups just like Haggis, while weeping copiously into my fur.

'Cata...'

'Darling, are you alright?' Her incoherent mumbling and tears brought George through. Laughing and crying at the same time, Mary could barely speak. 'Oh, George, he's come home. I knew he would!'

George didn't need to know who she meant; he swept us both into a bear hug. I was home.

They all came round then, the neighbours, upon one excuse or another; such was their affection for Mary that they had to share in her happiness. Small gifts were left for me: an extra creamy pint from the milkman...some expensive little trays of rabbit and green peas in jelly from the Oggs...a pheasant from old Jock.

Not everyone was pleased to see me, though.

Dogs have Masters, Cats have Staff

Dogs!

The first time I came face to face with a hostile dog was in the deep bracken behind the Mackie's cottage, down by the burn where it tumbles underground. The hound was a big beast; long legged and big boned, with a mean expression on its small-eyed face and a studded leather collar round its neck to mark its ownership. It was used to killing anything smaller than itself and was responsible for the much-lamented disappearance of Mr and Mrs Ogg's 'Fluffykins'. Well, he hadn't met a wildcat before.

Drooling muzzle to the ground, the hound snuffled loudly as it confidently followed my scent. I watched its foolish antics from the branches above until I grew bored. It had evidently been short-changed when it came to cunning and courage, and relied on its size to overwhelm its victims. Gathering my hindquarters and puffing out my tail so that I looked twice the size, I executed a faultless Drop From A Great Height, followed through by the Playful Introductory Rake. The feeble beast ran off, yelping loudly. Pitiful! Are dogs always this spineless? At least a badger puts up a decent fight! I went on the prowl to find a better opponent.

The postie made his rounds on his bicycle with his dog behind him. He had once been pecked on the bottom by a goose that had cornered him in Mr Jack's farmyard. Whenever they saw him, local children started honking and flapping their elbows like wings. Rumour was that he had never lived the embarrassment down. To stop it happening again, he had bought a dog. A mean-minded dog for a mean-minded man. Ambush was a Doberman with attitude, who terrorised the neighbourhood. He defended his territory against all comers, and his territory just so happened to be wherever he and his master were at the time. His owner took a perverse delight and pride in the misery his dog inflicted.

A heron-grey fog hugged the ground for days on end and refused to leave. Sounds were muted. The curlew called forlornly. Spiders busily spun their dew-pearled webs from blade to blade, waiting for the lazy yellow sun to burn through the mist and for the insects to rise into their nets. I drifted with the fog across tufted grass and heather, hunting rabbit and hare ~ sand and smoke through the grass. High above, the kestrel cried angrily as I took his rabbit.

The greenfinch-yellow fog lights of cars and bicycle were barely visible at six feet. People and creatures ghosted in and out of view. Spotting the perfect opportunity to make mischief, Ambush went for me, but I was no spoilt, sofa-soft moggie, no, not I! I jumped and twisted in the air, a perfect Grasshopper, followed by a lightning quick Double Rake and Disembowel, completed by a magnificent Red Squirrel Twist that barely kissed the postman's red cycle helmet before reaching the lower branches of a handy rowan. The dog yowled and turned to snap at me but I was safely out of reach by then. The postman swerved unnecessarily violently, I felt, and fell off. The shining Mercedes coming the other way swerved to avoid the wind-milling postman and crashed into the ditch.

'My new car!' the farmer cried, as he clambered from the ditch. 'What a catastrophe! You careless man!' He got out his mobile phone. 'John? Yes. Some eejit's run me into the ditch. I need...'

'My bicycle!' the postman groaned, running a hand through thinning hair. He peeled the mangled frame from the tree trunk and peered at the damage. I could see it well enough from where I hid. 'The front wheel is all bent and buckled,' he cried. 'What a catastrophe! How am I going to deliver the mail?' He looked at his heavy sack then back to the bicycle. 'What's the sorting office manager going to say about this?'

'He's going to say 'You should have looked where you were going' is what he's going to say,' the farmer was in no mood to listen.

'It was a big cat.'

'A big cat?' the farmer echoed sceptically, 'I don't see any cat. It must have been that big dog there. His owner ought to keep him under better control.'

'That's my dog!' said the postman, finally remembering the reason why he crashed. 'He wouldn't knock his master from his bike! Ambush, here boy.' Then he got back on track. 'It was huge,' the postman declared. 'Huge!' He held his arms out just so. Mmn. I must have grown fat indeed!

'It's your imagination, man, no cat's that big!'

'But I tell you…look at the scratches on my dog's back!'

'Just brambles, man!'

By the time the tractor arrived to pull the car out of the ditch, the fog had thinned to nothing and the pale sun revealed two men and a dog alone on the road. They were still arguing while local school children examined the crashed car with interest. By that evening everyone knew of the inexplicable catastrophe that had befallen the two men, and the rumour of a big cat.

It's a Catastrophe!

It was a perfect day for a prowl. A fresh wind chased cotton-wool clouds across the blue sky. The shepherd and his dogs chased flocks of woolly sheep across the lower pastures. By the time the Kirk bell shook sleepy heads out of their beds and into the bright summer morning, I had already dined on a half dozen voles and was heading back to the cottage, when a delectable scent diverted me.

A high pantry window was open at the back of one of the cottages. Even with my bad leg it was no trouble to jump from rubbish bin to the lower eaves and onto the window ledge. I stretched an experimental paw and pulled myself up and in. I landed between trays of eggs; a stack of goat's cheeses and two kippers laid out on a dish. All this was very tempting, I'm sure your own mouth is watering by now, but the magnificent object that took my attention was sitting cooling on a wooden board. It was a lot harder getting out again with my booty but I managed.

On the way home later on, I generously dropped the cleaned rib roast bones in the kennel just outside the cottage's back door. The name 'Archie' was painted in a sign over its door and it belonged to a black and white collie that spent most of its day chasing sheep – but not exclusively. Not so long ago, Archie had chased Haggis. Disgraceful; showed a shocking lack of respect for the elderly.

'Why, Mr Longbottom,' Mary opened the door to a wiry old man smothered by tweed, 'please, do come in.'

'Me and the Missus would like to invite you round for Sunday dinner.'

'Why, yes, we'd love to.' Mary had a genuine affection for the old couple and they for her.

'Herself has done a fine rib 'o beef with stovies for your man and she's been at that cookbook of hers for days to cook up something vegetarian for yourself. Seven o'clock?'

George smacked his lips in anticipation but he was to be disappointed. They were sharing a wee dram and eyeing the dining table with considerable interest when there was a kerfuffle through in the pantry. Mr Longbottom rushed to discover the cause of his wife's distress.

'What a catastrophe!' the old man cried with passion. 'Our dinner has been taken.' He looked bewildered. All eyes turned to where the dog contentedly lay, his nose and paws covered in crumbled earth. A search turned up the evidence buried at the bottom of a shallow hole next to his kennel. He was banished outside with no supper, although no one could explain how he got into the pantry. Oh, revenge is such a sweet dish. Only once had Mary glanced down with a twinkle in her eye, but I remained innocently curled by her feet.

26

'Well', she smiled when we returned from the Longbottoms. 'I think we finally know what to call you, puss.'

'Mary?' For once George did not follow her train of thought.

She laughed. 'I'm going to call him Catastrophe.'

Fortescue & Urquhart

Harvest was in. Tractors surrounded by squalling gulls ploughed the stubble fields, and winds swept up the falling leaves, depositing them in heaps. The postman puffed up the potholed road on his new bicycle and Ambush puffed behind him, now tied by a sturdy lead. The letters dropped through the letterbox and lay on the mat for a half-hour or so before George scooped them up on his way out to work. A packet of porridge oats covered them up and then The Scotsman. Finally, as the sun crested the hill, Mary looked at them.

'Fortescue & Urquhart' she whispered, staring at the creamy parchment envelope. Colour drained from her cheeks in sudden premonition. I have only seen such desperate stillness in a rabbit mesmerised by a stoat.

She opened it.

She went through half a box of tissues. She tried to ring George but he was teaching and his mobile was switched off. She left a message with his office. When her mobile didn't ring she tried again, but somebody hadn't passed the message on and now he was giving a tutorial.

She lifted the phone a half dozen times only to set it down again. Then, as if drawing on some past memory, she was suddenly all action. Colour flooded into her face and her mouth set in a thin determined line. Mary lifted the house phone. She had to key the number in twice, her fingers were shaking so. She bit her lips in fierce concentration. She tried five more times before someone answered.

'A-aunt Maud,' she said in a small voice. 'It's Mary. *Mary*. I just received a letter from Fortescue and Urquhart. Y-y-yes. Yes. No! But... why didn't you tell me she had taken such a bad turn? Well, yes, I know how difficult it's been over the past four months but...no, I'm not being selfish. It's just that we've hardly seen her this last year...I know that's what you told us, but I'm practically her daug-. But...she's my aunt! She told us she wanted us to visit. It's always you who -. No, no, of course I'm not trying to be difficult...all I wanted...I know she's your sister... Yes,' she was defeated. 'Of course we'll come.'

Bad News

George's motorcycle engine sounded like an angry bumblebee as he revved it up the pot-holed drive. Goodness knows how he didn't fall off.

'Mary?' his voice was still muffled by the helmet as he burst through the front door. I heard the bike fall off its side-stand outside.

'In here.'

In two strides he was at her side. 'Darling, what's wrong? I got your texts and several messages and I tried to ring but the phone was engaged.' He came to stand by her, anxiety in every movement. 'It's not...?'

Mary nodded, tears streaming down her face. 'A-a-aunt Edith, s-s-she's died! I thought she was doing so well, the doctor said so. But she's dead! She had a massive heart attack.' She handed him the crumpled letter. 'Aunt Maud never even told me! She says she was just so distraught it slipped her mind, but I don't believe her. The funeral is next Tuesday - and the w-w-will's to be read on November 3rd. And it says here to bring our costumes for the Hallowe'en Ball. How can they hold the Ball when Aunt Edith's just died?'

For once George didn't have an answer. He gently wiped away a tear with the back of a hand then wrapped her up in his arms. When she had quietened he took her for a walk beneath a black star-sprinkled sky and listened while she talked about her childhood with Aunt Edith.

The owl hooted.

The fox barked.

I padded along silently behind them.

Aunt Edith

In such a small community news travelled fast. Mrs Crombie, the tractor man's wife from down the road, was knocking on the door even before the postie arrived the next morning.

'Oh, goodness,' Mary frantically tried to tidy herself in the hall mirror. 'Look at the state of my face – it's all blotched and red.' True. And, after a sleepless night her eyes were so dilated they looked almost black. She looked like she'd been dragged through a hedge backwards, and believe me, having dragged lots of things through a hedge backwards, I have some small experience of the matter.

Mary let her friend in. Sympathy and a hug opened the floodgates again.

'We're g-going up tomorrow for my aunt's f-funeral on Tuesday,' Mary hiccupped as she made strong black coffee for them both. 'And then we're staying on till the W-will is read on 3rd November. The lawyers said that was Aunt Edith's wish.'

'Oh, Mary, chook,' the little woman laid a hand on her friend's arm. 'Oh, Mary, I'm so very sorry. You loved her very much, didn't you?' It was the right thing to say. Mary needed to talk it out. Her grief was as fresh and raw as the east wind.

Letting herself be guided to a chair by the fire, Mary sat silent for a few moments. I jumped softly onto her lap. Tears traced the contours of her face and dripped from her onto me, making my coat shiver with borrowed misery. She blew her nose loudly.

'She... When my parents and brother were killed she took me in, and then when she remarried I moved with her to Driechandubh. I was barely nine. She was like a mother to me. I spent eight happy years there,' she looked up at her friend. 'It's a magical place, Jane. The castle looks like something out of a fairy tale, as if it's grown out of the mountain itself.' Her voice softened with memories. 'George and I were married in the old Kirk on Chapel Isle, a small island on the loch in front of the castle. But then,' she hiccupped and her face crumpled, 'Aunt Edith had a mild heart attack and things have been going from bad to worse ever since.'

'I didn't realise she was so ill,' Jane shook her head.

'No! I didn't either! Last time we visited she seemed a little stronger. It was so difficult once she was bedridden to be alone with her. She was becoming so confused and Aunt Maud was always there, taking charge of everything as if she owned the place. Then late last year, just before Christmas, Aunt Maud moved in. She claimed Aunt Edith invited her, but Aunt Edith always detested her sister. After that, she refused to allow us to visit at all, saying Aunt Edith was not strong enough to receive visitors or take phone calls, and my letters were never answered. But then we got a letter from Aunt Edith asking why we hadn't come for so long. Well, Aunt Maud could hardly refuse us then,' she stared at the fire. 'But it got harder and harder to visit after that, and there were no more letters. Jane.' Twisting her hankie in her hand, Mary looked apprehensively at her friend. 'I know that this is going to sound far-fetched, but Aunt Edith said she'd written many times asking us to come but we never got the letters. I think Aunt Maud was stealing them.'

Jane weighed her answer quietly before replying. 'Did you suggest that to your Aunt?'

Mary nodded. 'But she just said that her sister was very ill and hallucinating. That she was just imagining she had written them.'

Jane considered Mary's answer carefully. 'That certainly sounds plausible. People who've had strokes are often confused. I mean,' she frowned. 'Why would she lie?'

Mary shook her head miserably. 'I don't know. But I am sure she is.'

Northwards

Haggis sat on the dusky rose brick wall beside the front gate and watched us go.

'You're much too old, puss, to come with us,' Mary had fondly scratched the old bag of bones under the chin. 'You don't like being away from home and we'll be back in two weeks.' The neighbours were going to see that she was properly fed and cared for, and the wood burning stove kept fed with wood for her comfort. But I was sad she was not coming with us. Haggis was part of my family now.

The gentle hills of Perthshire with their green woodlands and sheep-dotted farms gave way to lochs, then to wilder stands of pines and craggy heather-mantled moors. The trees were on the turn. Here the belly of the grey clouds hung low, hiding the mountains so that they loomed up, as if conjured by magic sprites. Herds of red deer lifted their dripping muzzles as we passed by and the osprey's keening cry carried on the wind. And still we headed north and west into the Highlands.

The Highlands are painted in subtle hues of rain and wind and rock. Their snow-capped mountains were created by ice then sculpted by storms. Red-berried rowan and silver birch climb the ragged rock-peppered gorges where snowmelt crashes down into the glens' heather-clad roots. The light is never constant, but ebbs and flows like the salty tidal lochs: mists mask ancient peat bogs and wreath the mountains so that every flower, every pine needle, every furred and feathered creature is pearled with moisture. Cold winds lament distant treacheries and the mists dance to haunted pipes. The old bones of the mountains hide their secrets and share them only with those who can speak the land's ancient language. These are the Highlands. This is my home.

Maniac!

It was a long drive. I catnapped on the back seat, head close to the open window, while they talked of the coming week with dread. Half an hour after setting off, the storm hit us with a curtain of solid water. The wind frayed clouds to dark ragged edges. Bridges of lightning arced across the sky. The wind's fingers rattled us around in the car like dice in a cup. A pheasant in the grip of the storm flew across our path – backwards. Leaves and feathers skirled in the golden headlights and were gone in the blink of an eye. The mountains were swallowed by the storm and coming night.

'Thirty more miles or so,' George said brightly, glancing at the satnav and then his wife. 'Ah,' he whispered as I opened one eye. 'OK, Catastrophe, quiet as we go.' Mary had fallen asleep.

The rain grew heavier.

Water tumbled down the dark mountainside in white-flecked torrents. Headlights flooded the car with bright white light as a car drew closer and closer behind us. Then the loud blaring of a horn shattered our sleepy composure.

'Maniac!' George cursed, as the fright jerked his arm hard to the left. Swerving, he avoided the ditch and had us back on course again, but in no time at all the strident horn blared out again.

'Lower your headlights, man,' George swore, struggling with the wheel as water coursed down from the mountainside and across the road. Rain foamed round rocks and pebbles. The sound of the horn filled our ears.

'I can't pull over here, the road's flooded! What's the idiot think he's doing? Look out!' In a roar and suggestion of red the growling car was past. Mud and stones rained down on the bonnet and windscreen.

Visibly shocked, George drew in at the next village. He sat back in the car seat. His hands were shaking and his mushroom-pale face floated in the dark.

'Good grief,' he let a deep breath out. 'That was close. Are you OK, sweetheart? I wish I'd got that idiot's registration number. I'd report him to the police. He could have run us off into the loch!' He lifted trembling hands from the wheel. 'Come on, Mary', he opened the door a crack. 'I need a strong coffee before we go any further. How about a hot chocolate for you?'

She nodded.

'Here, sweetheart,' her husband pulled a bright yellow jacket from the back seat. Being a large man in a small car he struggled into his own, cracking first elbow then fist on window and dashboard. There wasn't much choice, by now it was raining buckets outside. Mary put me on the floor at her feet and poured water into a dish. 'I think you'd better stay in the car.'

That was fine with me; I was already face down in a bowl of biscuits. Pulling up their hoods, they made a dash for it.

Driechandubh

The car turned from the main road.

'The south lodge, puss, we're nearly there.'

Its little engine revving hotly, gears clashing in protest, the car negotiated the loch-side road. Mud squelched and steam hissed as the car jarred and lurched forward by degrees.

'Dratted holes,' George complained as he tried and failed to get round a bone-jarring, rain-filled crater. The old car valiantly climbed its way out. The suspension groaned and the exhaust growled bad temperedly.

'I don't know why your Aunt Maud doesn't get the wretched things filled. It's not as if she's short of a bob or two. The place has gone downhill since we last visited.'

'I know, sweetheart,' Mary said soothingly, laying a pale hand on his shoulder. 'We'll just have to make the best of it. It won't be for long,' she added hopefully.

We passed through pinewoods, their aromatic scent invading the bubble of our car. Then woodland gave way to pasture and we picked up the edge of the loch again. Leaves touched to brilliance slammed against the glass. We turned a corner and for a split second the castle was imprinted on our eyes and memories. Lightning's fickle fingers explored towers and turrets and probed dark windows and darker doorways with splintered flashes of light. In the unkind clutches of the storm, Driechandubh was as dour and unwelcoming as its name. Few lamps beckoned visitors to that windswept castle or guided us through into the rain-lashed courtyard. No lights welcomed us at the great studded door. In their absence, the storm embraced us, etching every cobble, stone and turret starkly in white on black. The castle appeared to crouch hungrily over the water like a bloated toad, its pale tongue of a road leaping the moat and licking the loch side. Behind, hidden by the storm, loomed the mountains of the Dragon's Spine. Three vehicles lay parked across the driveway and forecourt, forcing us to stop beyond the shelter of the entrance arches. The rain grew even heavier.

Optimistically brandishing an umbrella, George got out. Wrestling one-handedly with the brolly, he rang the bell pull. Its voice was lost to the wind that howled like a stricken banshee. The treacherous umbrella turned inside out and sailed upwards into the darkness. The rain hammered down. George hammered on the door.

'That's strange', Mary murmured to me. 'Old Mr McFie's normally quicker than this. I wonder what the matter is?'

Turning up her hood and clutching me beneath her waterproof poncho, she got out to join her husband. He rang again.

'We'll have to try the side door,' Mary shivered. There was no protection from the storm as George knocked. This time he had more success.

'Who goes without?' a disembodied voice challenged above the keening cry of the wind. There was a short pause whilst George and Mary looked at each other in confusion at this unlikely greeting.

'That's not Mr McFie,' Mary said at last, as a choked gutter overhead gave way, dumping its contents upon our bedraggled gathering.

'Who goes without?' The high pitched voice repeated with a touch of irritation.

The rain hissed down.

The voice coughed meaningfully. The sound dragged all our eyes down to where a small hatch had opened barely five-foot from the ground. A nose poked out. The word parsnip sprang instantly to mind. It was attached to a rheumy eye that blinked owlishly as the spray caught it.

With water pouring down his neck, George was not at his best. 'We go without! Without an umbrella,' he answered, crossly kicking the studded oak. 'Now open the damn door, man. It's blowing half a gale out here!'

The small hatch was closed with a bad tempered thump. There was the sound of bolts being drawn. A chain rattled. High above, nestled between turrets and tumbling chimneys, an aged gargoyle gave its last gasp and toppled from the battlements.

The Storm

At first there was no sense of disaster. It simply looked as if an enormous hand had crumpled the car. The dull sound had been swallowed by the thunder. Only a ricocheting piece of masonry and a peppering of gravel chips gave the game away. Turning, George and Mary stood rooted to the spot, disbelief etched on their faces.

'Good grief, Mary', George uttered in a hoarse voice. 'That might have killed us!' He turned to where the door was slowly opening, the wedge of light illuminating the pitiful wreckage. Anxious to be out of the rain and danger, George put his shoulder to the heavy oak timbers. There was a muted 'ouff' and the sound of boots scraping unwillingly across a stone floor and we were in. The storm entered with us.

Chandeliers jangled in lively protest, their yellow light swinging crazily. Heavy banners and tapestries rippled and billowed. Getting stiffly to his feet and pointedly holding his nose, a small man peevishly dusted himself down. Muttering into his whiskers, he attempted to shut the door. George watched this unequal struggle for a moment before planting two large hands on the timbers. The door grudgingly closed, protesting mournfully every inch of the way. As they threw the latch, the boom and crash were banished behind four inches of oak and ten-foot thick stone walls.

'Dood evening, Sir, Dadam.' The small man bobbed his head like a dipper. 'Prune,' he offered, clutching his nose.

'Prune? No, no man. A towel would be more appropriate! And a brandy! My wife is chilled and shocked!'

'Tut.' The dour little man clicked his false teeth, almost losing them in the process. 'Prune, at dour service,' he persisted as he hung their dripping coats and ushered them to the fire that blazed in a huge hearth. 'Dou have bags...?' He flinched as the thunder boomed and I could see his reluctance to fetch their luggage from the car. He had no idea that there was a half-ton gargoyle embedded in the mangled wreckage.

'Let me get my wife to our room first,' George instructed him. 'Then we can take a look at the car.'

'As do wish, Sir.'

The odorous house was dim: darkly varnished floors and heavy curtains sucked in the light, hoarding it like a miser. A grand red-carpeted staircase swept us upward past two galleries and countless oil paintings and tapestries, and into a labyrinth of long damp corridors and stairways. It was a far cry from the light-hearted home of her youth that Mary had described. Prune's arthritic knees ensured we moved at a snail's pace. George fretted every step of the way, anxiously urging the wheezing butler forwards. Outside, the thunder boomed and cracked.

'But,' Mary was confused as we turned away from the main staircase. 'Aren't we in our usual room? Beside my...the room that used to be next to my Aunt Edith's apartments?'

'No, Madam. Mrs McGregor gave specific instructions for a room to be prepared on the fourth floor.'

Baffled at this break with tradition, Mary looked on the brink of tears as Prune finally opened a door and beckoned us in.

'Dour room, Madam, Sir. The bathroom is down the hallway.'

I padded in. It was freezing. My hackles instinctively prickled. I don't think we were expected to get this far.

Prune knelt and poked the fire in the grate into reluctant life, careful not to dirty his hands. A small flame licked the fibrous bricks of peat. The red glow started to warm the room.

'Your Aunt is in the Drawing Room, Madam. I will inform her you have arrived. Madam impressed upon me most urgently that you must not venture into the west wing. A chimney collapsed and it is in a very poor state of repair. Building work has been delayed until after the funeral.'

'Yes, yes,' George replied testily. 'No matter. My dear, a hot bath? You're chittering. Here,' he pulled off his damp jacket and wrapped it round her shoulders. 'Prune and I will go and retrieve what we can.'

'One moment.' Both Prune and her husband turned back to her. 'Whatever happened to Mr McFie? The... previous butler?'

'I'm sure I couldn't say, Madam.'

We both sat down near the fire. A feather of steam rose from her sodden shoes. We looked at our surroundings. The room was large enough, if a little bare. A four-poster bed tucked in beneath the eaves left room for little else save an armchair by the fire, a dresser and a cushioned window seat. The wind rattled the diamond-paned window. A dark tapestry decorated the wall. It smelt of mould and mothballs.

'Oh, puss,' Mary gathered me up. The chill air had reddened her rose-pink cheeks and nose. 'You don't like it either, I can tell.' She smiled thinly and set her shoulders squarely. 'Well, there's nothing for it'. She added two more bricks of peat and settled us down by the fire.

The melancholy rattle of rain on the windows matched our spirits. Elderly plumbing gushed and clanked as the bath slowly filled. True night fell outside. Nobody but the gargoyles noticed.

Aunt Maud

The winding stair led us down to a marble-floored hall, where a dusty grandfather clock ticked out its monotonous minutes.

Tick, tock... Tick, tock... Tick, tock...

George and Mary hesitated, but their hostess had been forewarned. A suit of armour swayed as an errant floorboard dipped. Yellow smoke billowed out the doorway, heralding the advance of Aunt Maud. Mary tried to smother a cough.

'Mary, dahling!'

Drenched in cheap perfume and dripping insincerity, Aunt Maud materialised out of the smog and flung her considerable self around her niece.

'What a perfectly *dreadful* accident!' she declared dramatically, waving her cigarette in the air. 'The storm is positively ferocious! But you are well and none the worse, Prune tells me!'

It was hard to tell her age beneath the larded layers of powder and rouge, but her clothes were all black satin and frilly lace to mark her mourning. It did not seem possible that such a delicate fabric could contain such a gargantuan creature. Smothered by an overwhelming bosom barely contained by a creaking whale-bone corset, Mary attempted to wriggle free. Observing his wife was in serious danger of asphyxiation, George stepped forward, reluctantly thrusting out a strong hand and painting a smile every bit as insincere as that of the hostess.

'My sincere condolences, Aunt Maud. How very... thoughtful of you to invite us to stay at such a unhappy time.'

We all knew it for a lie. Were it not for Fortescue & Urquhart, George and Mary would be none the wiser that Aunt Edith had died.

'Dear young man,' pale blue eyes sunk in a sea of cold porridge turned towards him. A nervous sheen of sweat beaded her head. I could smell fear beneath that false sweet scent that she had splashed on wrist and neck.

'Sooo delighted that you were able to make it in this awful weather!' she patted his hand patronisingly. 'It is so very sad,' she sniffed loudly, 'that it has to be upon the occasion of my *dear* sister's death.'

A lace handkerchief was whipped out as she made a great show, but behind it her small eyes were sharp and watchful. They alighted upon me.

'A cat.' Never had two words been so imbued with loathing.

'Yes,' Mary agreed, scooping me up protectively and for once I allowed it. 'He is a wildcat.'

The disagreeable face stooped over me, a patently insincere smile cracked the powder and rouge facade.

'Such a nice cat.' A sharp scratch beneath my chin belied her honeyed words but I was just as fast. The Gargantuan One withdrew her talons with a hiss and sucked her stricken finger. Without a word war was declared.

A sonorous gong sounded in the depths.

'Right,' Aunt Maud said briskly, gathering up her skirts and her niece. 'Dinner. I doo hope you like roast beef and suet pudding my dear?'

Her niece paled. 'Err, Aunt Maud,' she began reluctantly. 'I have mentioned before...you surely remember I - '

'What my wife is trying to say is that she is a vegetarian.' Her husband could be blunt when he chose to. 'How could you forget?'

But of course, Aunt Maud hadn't. 'A vegetarian?' she rolled the distasteful word around behind pursed red lips. 'How quaint, dahling. Are you really? Well, I'm sure Cook can find some vegetables to suit you. The turnip crop was good this year I hear.' She waved a hand enquiringly in Prune's direction.

'Tut. Very well, Madam.' His false teeth were in danger of falling out with pursed disapproval. Perhaps Cook was not well inclined towards fruit and vegetables. I followed Prune down to the kitchens where she proved herself well inclined towards cats. I had my fill of milk and slept beneath the blackened range.

Midnight

The clock had just struck twelve. They were all asleep now, cocooned in their blankets and quilts, these daylight creatures who dislike the dark so: the guests safely lodged in the east wing, Aunt Maud in one of the smaller chambers of the old keep. I doubt whether any other floor could hold her. But as they slumbered on, other residents awoke. How the Gargantuan One would squeal if she knew how many hundreds of four-legged and two-winged tenants she had hanging out in attic and cellar. Well, it was time to explore this vast castle and introduce myself to some of them. Time to discover its passages and hidden ways. Outside, the storm rattled the shutters and door, seeking a way inside. The wind's voice was hoarse from screaming. He must surely run out of breath soon. I stretched luxuriously and danced eagerly into the waking night.

The hunt was on!

The Trophy Room

I padded swiftly down the main staircase, past empty suits of clammy armour that stood permanently to attention with their axes and maces and quartered shields. On the last floor but one, before the entrance hallway, a huge painting hung on the wall. A great three-masted Spanish galleon in rough seas was being driven onto the rocks by kelpies that rose from the greenstone ocean deeps. Every time George passed it by, it piqued his attention.

The dove-blue slate in the entrance hall gave way to far older wooden floors that were cruelly pitted by the Gargantuan One's passage. She wobbled around on ludicrously high-heeled shoes that looked like they would snap at the slightest excuse. I easily followed her odorous trail in the general direction of the forbidden west wing. But no matter which corridor or corner I turned, I found the doors securely locked and barred, with signs demanding the wearing of hard hats due to scaffolding and roof repairs. Undeterred, I looked for an alternative and soon found it beneath the old dresser opposite the Gun Room. I squeezed through, then down beneath the floorboards where I caught supper before discovering a way out next to a huge fireplace. This large empty room covered with dust covers had the feel of a cave. The slightest noise echoed off emptiness. Dampness and decay folded in on itself and the mildewed house stretched away into darkness. Our entire cottage could have fitted in this one room with room to spare. I set off to explore.

I stood still, drawing the night deeply into my lungs, sifting its layers on my tongue, and examining each subtle shade of light and dark with my eyes. Every hair on my pelt is unique, resonating to the tiniest ebb and flow of the air. Satisfied, I padded lightly across the room, merely one shade of night amongst many. I went through room after room, each with its dust-covered furniture, fading gilt and empty yawning grates.

I had not been looking for Aunt Maud but I found her just the same. Strange, then, that I had not picked up her scent, for unlike me, people have to move by door and corridor and stair and I had picked up no spoor as I passed through the west wing.

Warmth and red light spilled out of this room, as well as low furtive voices.

'How could you miss?' I recognised the complaining tongue of the Gargantuan One. She was in a right crabbit mood. Fear and anger rolled spitefully off her tongue.

'I didn't miss!' her companion's gravelly tone was aggrieved.

'You know what I mean. They were already at the door! Crushing their car achieved nothing. Did you fall asleep?'

'Fall asleep! In this weather!? Look, it was pouring down and the wind was wailing like a banshee. I never heard the car arrive at all. You weren't up there, Maud, you've no idea how bad it was.'

'That was the whole point of the exercise, wasn't it, Douglas?' she responded sarcastically. 'An old castle…a geriatric old butler who didn't make it to the door in time…a wild storm. An unfortunate accident! Driechandubh passes to the next beneficiary in the Will, namely me! End of story!'

'Damned inconvenient the old lady dropped dead before I'd had time to switch both copies of the Will,' the man complained peevishly, 'If you'd not given her such an overdose of doctored tea, none of this would be necessary. Puts us in a bit of a fix, what, what?'

'It wouldn't have if you had done your job properly today,' the Gargantuan One snapped. 'We'll not get many chances to try again before the Will is read.'

'Well, if we don't we'll fall back on plan B and switch the lawyer's copy of the Will, too, when he arrives. That's all,' the man said. 'I'm an excellent forger if I say so myself. No one will be able to tell the difference, Maud, I promise. And think of the reward – Driechandubh itself! No more penny-pinching. Should finance your London home and my lifestyle for a long time to come!'

'That's all very well,' Aunt Maud snapped. 'But the longer they're here, the more chance there is of them accidentally finding out what we were up to, like McFie did! Mary grew up in this castle, you know. She might spot some missing paintings or Chippendale furniture.'

'What?' the man scoffed. 'With all this wealth? The house is huge and positively stuffed with antiques. I can hardly spot the missing ones, and I stole them! Well, you'll just have to tell them again that this wing's unsafe, that's all, and they will never know. There's scaffolding all over the place after I loosened that chimney, so they won't find it hard to believe. Say the roof is unsafe. It's hardly a lie. After their near miss today, they'll take it to heart. And once the Will is read, they'll be out of here for good. And so will we, thank heavens! It's in the middle of nowhere!!'

The Gargantuan One grunted doubtfully. 'I don't know anything about her husband ~ he may be harder to fool.'

'Oh, good grief! He's only an academic isn't he, Maud? Point him towards the Library. It's one of the best private collections in the world. He'll have his nose in foosty old manuscripts so fast he'll never notice anything. And you've said she's as timid as a mouse. What's there to worry about?'

Interesting. So, Aunt Maud was not all she seemed. That paint and rouge hid more than a sagging face and a sharp tongue. What secrets did she and her companion hide? Curiosity was nearly my downfall. Nudging the door open, I flowed in with the shadows. Cigarette smoke coiled and eddied around me. It lay thick on the ground. The stench was vile and masked what lay beneath, so what happened next found me unprepared. The light of the fire gilded chair and table and much more. They were all here, my brothers and sisters from the woodlands and many more besides, arrayed around the wall or on pedestals. The tawny owl with wings spread and talons clawing at the air. The twelve point stag. The mountain hare in his winter coat. All rigid, frozen forever, their unseeing eyes made bright by the fire. It was their utter silence that stopped me in my tracks. Where is the honour in such trophies?

I turned and fled.

Where's Mr McFie?

'Where's Mr McFie?' Mary asked as she sat down to breakfast with a bowl of porridge. 'I haven't seen him about. And how long has Prune been here?'

'I dismissed him two months ago,' Aunt Maud answered absently. She was reading the financial pages in The Scotsman, jotting down numbers on a piece of paper.

'*Dismissed him*?' Mary put her spoon down. 'Why on Earth would you do that? He's been devoted to Aunt Edith for twenty years. He knows her wishes and this castle like the back of his hand.'

44

'Exact... I mean,' Aunt Maud belatedly paid attention. 'He was never punctual.'

'Never punctual?' Mary's eyes widened in disbelief. 'But he was in the army for twenty years. He's regular as clockwork.'

'He... he was... dishonest.'

Mary just looked at her.

Aunt Maud galloped full tilt into the silence. 'Yes, dishonest. I caught him stealing... your Aunt's quaich collection.'

'But it was *his* collection. He was her piper, after all. She gifted one to him each and every year, on the night of St Andrew's day.'

'Really? Forgive an old lady, dahling. I'm just getting a tad confused. Ah, yes!' Inspiration struck. 'Now I remember. He was drinking heavily.'

'Drinking heavily? But he hardly touched a drop! Aunt Edith would never have dismissed him.'

'Well, my dahling,' said Aunt Maud spitefully. 'She isn't here anymore, is she? And life has to get on. I've an estate to run now, I mean in the interim. You've no idea what hard work that is, you've no experience of these weighty matters,' she added condescendingly. 'I've an estate to run and a Ball to organise and I'm just doing the best an old lady can. I'm sure Edith would understand.'

'No she would not!! Never!' Mary retorted heatedly. 'You didn't have the right to sack him! You are not legal owner of Driechandubh. And how can you hold the Hallowe'en Ball less than a week after she's buried? The Will won't have been read. Until then Driechandubh still belongs to her. No one else has the right to host the Ball!'

Aunt Maud stood, her eyes narrowing threateningly. With no witnesses her mask was slipping. 'I'll have you know, little Miss,' she hissed. 'That Edith insisted, yes, my dear sister insisted that the Ball was to go ahead, no matter what. A Wake, she said, so that all her friends could celebrate her life. No, my dear, the Ball is going ahead just as she would have wished! And until the Will is read, Madam, I will make all the decisions around here whether you like it or not!'

Her mouth a tight line, Mary stood up and put her napkin down. 'Come on, puss. I need some fresh air.'

Cook

Cook was footering about the kitchen, loudly humming a ditty. Apart from her fondness for cats I had learnt that she came from the Isle of Lewis in the Western Isles. She spoke with a lilting singsong voice that softened her speech.

'Och, there you are now,' the little woman swept Mary up in a floury kiss. 'With himself.' She showered me with flour although I avoided the kiss. 'Och, you're covered with cobweb, now. Where have you been?' Cook ruffled my fur but I ducked out of reach. 'He's probably been exploring all those tunnels and hidden passageways, bless his little heart.'

She turned back to Mary. 'And how was your churney, child? It was a tirty tay to be triving, now, wasn't it? Chust you come in now. Come in.'

She was a blethering, bustling bantam of a woman, with apple cheeks and bird-bright eyes, who never seemed to pause to draw breath as she shooed Mary towards a chair by the range.

'I'm well, Mrs Anderson,' Mary smiled wanly. 'I - '

'Why child, you're looking awfy wabbit and pale. You've been weeping!' Cook tilted Mary's head to the light.

'Oh, Cook!' Mary's face crumpled.

Anxiously clucking and crooning like a mother hen, Cook wrapped Mary up in affection. 'Wheesht, child, wheesht. I know it's hard to accept she's finally gone, but she'd been awfy ill these last six months now.'

'It's j-j-just I never had a chance to say goodbye. I've hardly seen her this last few months and Aunt Maud never even told us she had died!'

Cook's face made it plain what she thought of Aunt Maud.

'She's a wicket woman, right enough,' she agreed. 'Wicket! Tings have not been right this last while with Herself being so ill.'

'What sort of ti-things?'

'All sorts of tings, child. I'm not one for gossip, but...'

For one not given to gossip, Cook did remarkably well.

'Now,' Cook said firmly, producing a box of tissues from thin air. 'Chust try your eyes. We can't be letting your Aunt have the satisfaction. I've chust this very minute made some bannocks, your favourite,' she deftly whisked the smoking griddle from the range. 'And here's some of Mr Anderson's honey; none to match it in all of Braeside.' She heaped round oatcakes on the plate despite Mary's protestations.

'And I'm not forgetting himself.' She moved to the huge kitchen sink. 'Here's a bowl of cullen skink left over from dinner,' she placed a dish in front of me.

Cullen skink? It certainly sounded like something the cat dragged in. It turned out to be a heavenly mix of milk and smoked fish that could have been conjured up for cats. I purred my appreciation and had to admit to you that I had been getting a mite peckish and was contemplating one of Aunt Edith's geese or a plump peacock. Cook scratched my chin. Fat and full I rolled over.

'Why, Mrs Anderson,' Mary was amazed. 'He's rarely affectionate like that.'

Cook harrumphed. 'In that case, I'm bound he'll be avoiding Mrs McGregor.' It wasn't a question. 'She'd have him made into a coat in no time at all. But he'd have loved your Aunt Edith, she always had a way with the wild animals, chust like yourself.'

Mary nodded in fond remembrance. 'She did, didn't she?'

It's Cold Outside

'Here, sweetheart,' George handed his wife her hat and gloves and scarf. 'Wrap up warmly, it's freezing out there. We haven't all got fur coats.' He grinned at me as he took her arm. 'So how was Cook?' he asked, as Mary led us out through the pantries and sculleries and past the old servants' quarter to the tradesmen's entrance at the side of the castle.

Mary drew in a sad breath. 'She puts on a brave face, but underneath she's just as devastated. She and Aunt Edith became firm friends when Aunt Edith married step-uncle Hamish,' she remembered. 'Cook helped Aunt Edith enormously during the first couple of years to get used to being mistress of such a huge estate. She's normally not got a bad word to say about anyone, but she said things went from bad to worse once Aunt Maud moved in eleven months ago. None of the staff could get near Aunt Edith, and Aunt Maud gradually started making all the decisions, although she said she was merely carrying out Aunt Edith's wishes. The castle was closed to visitors and tourists. Aunt Edith's friends were turned away by Aunt Maud, who insisted she was always too ill. Nobody believed her. But what could they do? When they questioned some of her decisions, Aunt Maud started sacking staff who've worked here for years.' Mary blew her nose loudly. 'Jamie Peat and Katie Moran were the first to go, then Mr McFie...'

'I know, sweetheart, Aunt Maud's such a vile old harridan.' He stopped to tenderly brush away a tear from Mary's cheek. 'It's hard to believe they were sisters!'

'She's a total baggage!' Baggage was one of Mary's favourite insults. She could invest that one word with a wealth of emotion. Hearing her, a scurrying maid turned back in surprise as we passed through the slate-flagged corridors and out into the bright, new-minted day. Her husband also looked at Mary in surprise. She was normally such a gentle creature, but now there was a quiet rage boiling beneath the surface.

There was a hushed stillness to the air as if the elements had finally come to their senses. The storm had taken itself south, leaving a trail of wreckage in its wake. The sound of ripsaws buzzed through the morning air like angry bees, as the foresters tried to clear the estate roads. The sea loch that swept round one side of the castle to form a natural defence on three sides was flat as a mirror, the swell of the distant tides barely visible. Nature was clearly exhausted. We walked round the side of the east wing to the long driveway, where it swept down from the castle entrance to the moors beyond.

Washed out paddocks on either side were dotted with ruminating sheep and long-coated Highland cattle the colour of honey. Where they congregated, steam rose in the cold air in a flatulent haze.

'Come on!' Mary cried, swept up by memories of childhood. We followed at a statelier pace, passing between the boulders that burrowed up through coarse grass and heather. The call of a curlew dipped across the water, a lonesome goose-pimpling cry that made them shiver. Bracken, burnished to copper by the low winter sun, sprinkled the grass with amber fire.

Having reached a stile, Mary turned to look back at the castle. In the softer light of day, Driechandubh was every inch the fairy-tale castle she had promised. A grand affair of white turrets and towers hedged about by thick-walled baileys and girdled by snow-capped mountains. Inside, it was positively bursting at the seams with cubby-holes and corridors, hidden passageways and priest holes, grand stairs and armouries, drawing rooms and music; beneath the floorboards and down in the cellars and vaults lay all manner of wonderful mysteries.

George irritably slapped his arm and then scratched his head. Mary sucked in a deep breath. A cloud of insects made her cough.

'Midges,' her husband growled. 'I thought they'd be long gone by this time of the year. Let's move away from the water.'

They wandered through the woods in companionable silence. I left them to it and was half way through lunch when they came upon me.

'Catastrophe!' Mary was shocked. 'That's one of...was one of Aunt Edith's prize geese.' Wide-eyed she looked up at George.

'Not any more, it isn't,' George laughed. 'You've got to get used to it, Mary. He may curl up on your lap but he's as wild as heather at heart. Talking about goose, I'm getting a little peckish.' He turned his wrist. 'It's nearly half twelve. I wonder what Cook's prepared for lunch?'

As if reading his thoughts, a distant bell sounded. We turned back and had just cleared the woods when a red car roared up the drive, impatiently hooting at the gangs of tractors and foresters blocking its way.

George frowned. 'I wonder...' he mused suspiciously as the sports car veered onto the lawn, and swept up to park beneath the castle entrance in a dramatic cloud of gravel and dust. 'That sounds awfully like the car that nearly ran us off the road, and it's the right colour, too!'

The Duke of Cairngorm

'Mary, dear, doo let me introduce you to an old friend of your Aunt's, the Duke of Cairngorm.'

A knife of a man unfolded out of the armchair.

'No need to call me, Your Grace,' the Duke gripped George's hand and then Mary's. 'Just plain Douglas will do,' he smiled condescendingly. 'We're all friends here.'

So... this was Aunt Maud's mysterious guest of the previous evening. All elbows and angles, with eyes as sharp as his nose. Approaching middle age, he was dressed in loud tartan trews and tweed. His shoes and belt buckle gleamed. The russet thatch he wore on his head looked like a badly made crow's nest that had dropped from a great height, but the man preened like a cock pheasant. A vain creature, then, and perhaps as empty headed. I stored that information for future use. Always know your enemy.

'Charmed,' the Duke held onto Mary's hand a little too long. She snatched it back. George's eyes narrowed and his mouth set in a hard line. So did the Duke's. Sensing her master's displeasure, the overweight, wrinkled terrier hanging at the Duke's heels growled and lunged. I was getting fed up with dogs, so didn't mess around. A lightning quick Spit & Rake was instantly followed by Smother & Disembowel. You could hear her squealing all the way down the long corridor, paws skittering in her haste to get away. Now she knew who was really in charge.

Red faced with anger, the dog's owner bit down hard on whatever comment he was going to make and fixed a smile on his face before turning back to Aunt Maud's guests.

'Charming,' the Duke said, red moustache quivering with rage. 'Your cat, I take it?'

'Yes,' Mary smiled sweetly. 'He is!'

Prune clattered out with the desert plates. Hidden by the damask linen tablecloth, I was chewing on a slice of pork George had slipped under the table. As the Gargantuan One served coffee, Mary cleared her throat.

'How long did you know my aunt...Douglas?' A seemingly innocent question but it had a hard edge. My ears twitched.

'Oh, a long time, my dear.' Waving his hand in the air, the Duke neatly avoided her question. 'Years and years,' he added vaguely, as if time would divert Mary from her course. I could smell his sour anxiety and wondered if Mary could. Furless-ones have no nose for such things.

'Strange,' Mary smiled sweetly but I could sense she had her hackles up. 'She never mentioned you once, in fact, in all the time I've lived and visited here I've never met you. Strange, don't you think?' George glanced at his wife in surprise.

The Duke had ferret eyes that darted furtively from side to side in appeal to Aunt Maud. 'Ah, well, err, I – We, err, used to go shooting together, don't you know? In your Aunt's younger days. On my estate at Cranbruik and – Ow!'

'But, dahling,' the Gargantuan One waddled hastily over from the sideboard tramping on her co-conspirator's foot, coffeepot in hand, a fey light in her eye. Instinct took over. I slipped from Mary's lap. 'You know how dear Edith's memory was failing her. She was always forgetting things. It was Douglas, after all, who alerted me to your Aunt's failing health a year ago. Oh, dear!' She drew back as her niece cried out and rose to her feet, hot coffee spilling from her lap. Mary's chair clattered to the floor. 'Clumsy me,' Aunt Maud cried. 'And *so* hot!' Grasping the water jug she emptied the contents on her niece who cried out a second time. 'And on your best skirt, too. Prune, please escort my niece down to the kitchens and see if Cook can't do something to get the coffee stain out.'

'No matter,' George's tone was clipped and tight with anger. 'I shall see to my wife.' He ushered her out without a backward glance. I chose to stay beneath the table, forgotten.

'Don't you think that was a little obvious, Maud?'

'And you weren't, Douglas?' she snapped angrily. 'You'd have given the game away if I hadn't intervened. Shooting indeed! Edith was weak and feeble like my niece. Animals are on this earth to eat or wear, but Edith treated them like friends and companions. Pigs! Geese! Cats and dogs everywhere. Always rescuing some wretched creature or other. Donating absurd sums to animal charities. Well, I got rid of them all and put a stop to that. Nasty smelly creatures.'

'*I* got rid of them all,' the Duke corrected her. 'In my landrover. Dumped them in the middle of the moor'.

He did, did he? And as for her ~ nasty smelly creatures indeed! She'd regret those words before our visit was over. I slipped out and left them squabbling like pheasants.

'I *really* don't like him,' Mary sat wrapped in towels as her husband raked up the smouldering fire and added bricks of peat. 'We don't like him do we, puss? Not one bit. And Aunt Edith never went shooting in her life! She loved animals…Come to think of it, where are her cats and dogs? Where are they all? And the pigs: Hamlette and Omelette? We never saw them down in the loch field, did we?' Doubt was beginning to creep into her voice. He looked up at her husband.

I cringed. I think we ate Hamlette for lunch… If her husband had the same thought he kept it to himself.

'Oh, George, you don't suppose... they've been put down, do you? She wouldn't do that, would she?'

'Oh yes, she would,' he replied thoughtfully. 'Oh yes, I can imagine Aunt Maud doing just that.'

They looked at each other in stunned silence.

New Staff

Dinner was a fairly frosty affair although the food itself was marginally warmer than it had been at lunch. This was due to the arrival of a new footman who moved at an altogether faster speed than poor old Prune.

The afternoon had nearly worn away when I had spotted Prune entering the Drawing Room with a smartly dressed young man. He was an ordinary looking boy with hair the colour of a fox in winter, penetrating blue eyes and a double helping of freckles. Downstairs, Cook had welcomed him warmly with hugs and tears in equal measure, though I didn't fully understand why. It seemed that he was born in the village and some family loss had recently brought him back home unexpectedly.

Curled around a strategically located pot plant on the landing, hidden from the Gargantuan One's predatory eyes, I watched as the boy drew himself quietly to attention while Prune introduced him. Aunt Maud gave his references a quick glance before tossing them carelessly on the table.

'So, you think you can cope with the job of junior footman?'

'Aye, Ma'am.'

Ma'am! Not just plain old Mrs McGregor anymore! Aunt Maud liked that immensely, oh, yes she did. She positively wriggled like an eel with delight.

'So...' there was no serious interest, this was just another tedious task. 'Your most recent employer was?'

'I've been in service to Lady Marwarbler of Hedgerow Hall, but I had tae come hame. Me mam's richt poorly. Taken a bad turn she has, and me Da's long since passed away. And me - '

'Yes, yes,' she responded testily. The mere mention of the aristocracy had already clinched it. 'You'll do.' She waved a negligent hand. 'I'll employ no shirkers now, mind, or you'll be sent packing immediately. Away with you. Yes, yes, off you go. Prune will instruct you as to your new duties.'

'Ma'am?' Prune enquired, as the boy headed down to the kitchens.

'He seems satisfactory,' the Gargantuan One conceded, grudgingly. 'Pity he can't speak plain English.'

Mirror, Mirror on the Wall...

With no dogs to play with, I was hunting an arthritic old rat that had managed time and time again to elude me. She was a bony, scarred old creature, probably not worth the eating, but a worthy foe and matriarch of a clan of thousands. For a black rat she was huge, and her one milky-blind eye did not slow her down. Canny and cunning, she knew the cobwebbed world beneath floorboards and behind wood panelling like the back of her paw. I'd caught and disembowelled dozens of her offspring and minions, but she escaped me every time. I was in the east wing following a promising lead beneath the floorboards when a strange crooning sound reached my ears; similar to the contented sound of eider ducks on the sea lochs in summer. Curiosity aroused – it is after all in my nature – I peered through a mouse hole in the skirting boards.

Even though the day was still overcast, three twelve-pane windows gave plenty of light to see by, and they revealed the strangest thing. Aunt Edith's large bedroom looked as if an autumn storm had breached the castle walls. Wardrobe doors swung on their hinges, drawers were pulled fully out and the gaping mouth of a small wall safe hung darkly open. Designer clothes and shoes and hats lay scattered everywhere. And nestled contentedly in the middle of this magpie's nest, surrounded by silver brushes and jewellery, sat Aunt Maud.

Mirror, mirror on the wall…
Who's the plumpest of them all?

She was gazing into the oval dressing-table mirrors so that she could see her face not only once but three times. Her hands were caressing silks, examining diamonds and shimmering pearls that spilled out of carved velvet-lined boxes, trying on designer shoes that were far too dainty for her over-sized feet. Cinderella's ugly sister would most definitely not be going to the ball in those!

She was muttering and cursing as she stood up, first to try this necklace, then another. Tiaras and brooches brought feral smiles. Earrings selected, she took another half-hour to find a bracelet that would fit round her doughy wrist, but the rings eluded her. First square-cut rubies followed by smoky Cairngorms, sapphires and amethysts were flung at the fireplace as she failed to get one, then the other onto fingers the size of white pudding sausages – a new delicacy that Cook had introduced me to.

The old lady lying in the family crypt wasn't yet buried, but Aunt Maud was already picking over the bones.

Can you Imagine?

The sounds of silver teaspoons tinkled in fine bone china. All was serenity and refined sensibilities. The Gargantuan One was entertaining seven exquisitely dressed ladies for afternoon tea, in the elegantly appointed front drawing room. I was draped over the back of an armchair by the cheery fire, indistinguishable from the fur stoles that hung limply around elegant powdered shoulders. How did they think they could look beautiful wearing dead creatures for fashion? Could they not hear the screams? Not the see the blood that stained them?

'Three sugar lumps, your Ladyship?' Aunt Maud simpered, eying their furs with an envious eye.

That disagreeably faced lady, weighed down by strings of pearls and a generous helping of bosom inclined her head ever so slightly, diamonds flickering from a jewelled and feathered fascinator in her hair. I was fascinated by it and contemplated playing with it.

'And how many for you, Dame Inversnekkie?'

'Why two, thank you.' Dame Inversnekkie's diamond brooch and necklace caught the light.

'Mai dear,' a third guest raised her elegantly plucked eyebrows and considered her hostess down the length of a hooked nose and pince-nez glasses. 'How are you coping? Ai mean, the inconvenience of organising a charity ball at this very difficult time...You are very brave to continue despite your bereavement...You say it was dear Edith's wish?'

Aunt Maud graciously inclined her head, mimicking those around her like a magpie. 'Of course, you will all be attending?' she simpered. 'Edith particularly mentioned you, her dearest friends? Which is why ai invited you round for afternoon tea. To discuss those charities most deserving of our efforts this year.'

'Of course, my dear,' there were murmurs of assent.

'And ai understand you have recently had trouble with staff!' a plump lady in a glittering designer confection enquired. 'How do you manage?'

'Well,' Aunt Maud held back imaginary tears. Rubies flashed from her ears with borrowed firelight. 'One always does one's best in trying circumstances.'

'Qwait so, qwait so.' There were knowing nods as they digested the wisdom of that statement, along with a fruit scone and clotted cream. I doubted they would know a trying circumstance if they fell over one.

'And were you close to your sister, my dear?'

'Oh, yes! Countess,' Aunt Maud trilled, popping a morsel of cake into her accommodating mouth, barely dropping a crumb on her mink stole. 'We were quite inseparable! Ai'm quite inconsolable.' Out came another lace handkerchief.

May she choke on that lie or that crumb of cake!

There was a short respectful silence then matters turned to other topics.

'You know Lady Bamsburgh, my dear?'

'Whai no,' Aunt Maud conceded after a moment's hesitation. 'Whai do you ask?'

'Well, my dear, quite the scandal!! The old boy finally died and the poor creature found that there was no money! He'd gambled it all away in Monaco, leaving her with huge debts.'

'No money!!???' they chorused like starlings.

'Imagine...'

There was a short silence. Evidently their imaginations weren't up to it.

'So,' the Gargantuan One clapped her hands in ghastly childlike fashion. 'Doo tell!'

'Well, the Darcys had just broken off Beatrice's engagement to the eldest son, Robert – ai mean, no money! – And Harrods had refused her any further credit, when she had the most amazing stroke of luck. Some distant relative in Argentina died and left her ten million dollars.'

'Whai,' Aunt Maud swallowed her envy with a crumb of chocolate cake and fluttered her eyelashes. One fell off into the strawberry jam where it lay like a swatted fly. 'As ai said only the other day to Baroness Blackthorn, such thoughtful relatives are a scarce commodity these days. I mean, dearest Edith, may she rest in peace, recklessly spent most of dahling Herbert's money on animal charities and foundations. Between you and me, there is very little to inherit, so ai might be forced into selling and retiring to our London house with a little apartment in Monte Carlo, ai think. Ai have the very property in mind'

Oh, one did, did one?

The Family

It had been a long walk, meandering in the autumn sunshine. We had taken the track as it wound west and north through rowan and birch to the foot of Buchaille Dubh Mor, the imposing mountain that guarded the entrance to Glen Dubh. Turning westward, we watched a heron fish in a deep pool where snowmelt threw itself from the mountainside in a tumble of waterfalls. The shadows were lengthening and it was growing cold. The wind smelt of snow.

'It's nearly five already!' George sighed. 'Probably time we were heading back. The evenings are drawing in so fast.'

Mary nodded, clearly as reluctant as her husband was. Their wrecked car had been towed away after breakfast, leaving them wretched and disheartened. Euphoria over our narrow escape had given way to shock, as they realised just how much they had lost. There was simply no money to replace the old car, nor their ruined belongings. They'd managed to salvage one battered suitcase and George's kilt and sporran, but the rest was pulverised. Debris from the shattered gargoyle was still being raked up as we walked up garden steps guarded by weathered stone griffins and onto the upper gravel driveway.

'Ohh,' George sucked in a sharp breath, as we neared the front of the house where two cars were parked next to the Duke's post-box-red TVR. 'An Aston Martin Vanquish DB7!' he ran his hand over the gleaming, midnight-blue car parked in the entrance. 'And a McLaren F1. Good thing the gargoyle didn't drop on any of these! The cost would be horrendous!' His smile faded and he turned to his wife. 'Family?'

Mary nodded with a look of resignation. 'Family.' She pulled a long face.

'George – '

'I know,' he smiled grimly and nodded. 'Try not to lose my temper. Are they really so obnoxious?'

The Heron

'Mary, dearest,' a young woman in a white lacy confection that sparkled flounced down the huge red-carpeted staircase. She had the highest heels I had ever seen; they were like an extra pair of legs. Wearing a short cut, grey-feathered jacket and brandishing a bright yellow handbag, she reminded me of the grey heron I had seen the day before fishing in the moat. The Heron held Mary in a delicate embrace and pecked '*mwu mwu.*' like some bird mating ritual above my fur as I lay curled about Mary's neck. About Mary's age, she was all frills, flounces and feathers with a flawless peachy complexion. But her leaf-green eyes were cold as ice in mid-winter.

'I'm so sorry, Georgina,' Mary offered, dutifully accepting the superficial kiss from glossy ruby lips that barely grazed her cheek, hoping no doubt I would not react.

'Sorry, darling?' the Heron tilted her head quizzically to one side. The matching yellow feathers on her tiny box hat swayed enticingly.

'Your step-mother...' Mary was incredulous.

'Oh! Yes, yes of course,' the Heron nodded her blond curls. 'Step-mama. Yes, such a pity, but I'm sure it was her time to go... Oh!' Her greedy eyes lit up. 'What a perfectly lovely stole. Such smoky colours! Such a glorious thick tail! Where did you get that, darling? Harrods? Maceys? Venice?'

'He's not – '

The Heron poked me with an impeccably manicured and polished fingernail. I hissed and whipped my tail in warning. It was probably the first time that she had encountered fur still attached to its original owner. The Heron screamed and swung her handbag. George stepped between us with a raised arm and neatly fielded bag and fist.

'Catastrophe is one of the family,' he firmly lowered her arm. 'And I'm Mary's husband, George.'

'Charmed, I'm sure,' the Heron said huskily. Planting a red kiss on his cheek, she slipped her arm through his, doubtless to prevent him from running away. 'Do come and tell me about yourself,' she led him off to the morning room, leaving us in the hall.

Mary, anger sparking in her earth-brown eyes, trailed behind. I slunk along behind her. I had no wish to find myself a part of that detestable woman's wardrobe.

How Very Frightful!!

The normally placid lounge rang to the sound of loud confident voices.

'Stanley, don't you know, frightfully nice to meet you.' A tall man going to fat bounced himself off the deep sofa with a grunt, and reached forward to grasp George's free hand with an even larger one.

'Just flown over from New York, don't you know?' The ice tinkled in his crystal tumbler. 'Took a frightful age to get here. This place is just in the middle of nowhere! No idea why Daddy ever bought it. Plane to Edinburgh then a frightful little plane to Inverness and then I had to hire a car. Dashed taxi driver refused to come all this way.'

Mary tried to muster a sympathetic tone and failed. 'Really? How frightfully dreadful.' That earned her a sharp glance but she was all innocence.

A loud voice drawled. 'Step-cousin, Mary.' Its owner, a tall powerfully built young man dressed in cashmere, tweeds and kilt strode forwards from the drinks cabinet. You could see the two men were brothers.

'Crispin...'

'Ah,' Crispin said, spotting Mary's quizzical expression as her voice trailed off. 'Yes, I thought I would ... you know...dress as the locals do. When in Rome do as the Romans do and all that. Frightfully quaint, don't you think? After all,' he smiled smugly, 'As the eldest son I am going to be Laird here, aren't I? Have I captured the right tone, do you think?' He offered Mary a kiss that missed entirely, before twirling. As he spun round he came face to face with George, who had freed himself from the Heron's hot clutches.

'And you are...?'

'George,' drawled George. 'Frightfully pleased to meet you, old chap.'

Shipwrecks and Salmon

'So, George,' Crispin waved a fork loaded with salmon in the air, causing Prune to step back smartly before his bewhiskered nose was stabbed. 'What do you do with yourself? Business? Finance? Stocks & Shares?'

'No, no, nothing like that. I teach Maritime Archaeology and History at Stirling University.'

'Really?' Crispin was barely listening. He was eyeing up the coat of arms that hung above the fireplace. 'How frightfully exciting! Err...'he turned back to George. 'What exactly *is* maritime archaeology, old chap?'

'It's how we learn about history from maritime finds, generally shipwrecks.'

'Gosh!' the Heron gushed. 'Shipwrecks! Sooo romantic!!' Laying a beringed hand on George's, she fluttered her eyelashes at Mary's husband. 'Does that mean you actually dive down to wrecks? Like James Bond!'

George pointedly removed his hand and used it to pick up his crystal wineglass. The ruby wine caught the candlelight, throwing his hawk's eyes into sparks and shadows. 'Yes,' he took a sip. 'Whenever I can get the opportunity. But mostly I research and teach.' He reached across to squeeze Mary's hand.

'So,' Aunt Maud maliciously twisted the knife, knowing the answer full well before she asked the question. 'You're a professor, then?'

'No,' George's eyes were hard as flint as he met her disdainful challenge. 'I'm a humble Senior Lecturer.'

Aunt Maud yawned rudely and picked her teeth. Senior Lecturers and shipwrecks obviously held no interest for her. Food did. Her eyes lit up as Campbell served saddle of venison.

The Writing Business

'So...' Smarting from her rebuff, the Heron unsheathed her manicured claws. 'How's the writing business these days?' she smiled spitefully at Mary. 'Are you on the Times Best Sellers list yet?'

Mary smiled thinly as Prune placed a cheese soufflé in front of her. 'I'm not quite ther- '

'Who's your publisher?' the Heron cut across Mary's answer. 'Harper- Collins? Bloomsbury? Penguin? Corgi...?' She let the question hang in the silence.

'I'm not actually pub- '

Stanley belched, spraying the table with crumbs. 'Ooops, pardon!' he shrugged apologetically.

'I'm self-published...' Mary's voice was so quiet they had to strain to hear.

'Self-published?' The Heron invested those two words with distaste as if she had just found a slug in her lettuce. 'So you don't have an agent or publisher?'

'No.'

'Oh, dashed bad luck,' gravy dribbled down Crispin's chin. He wiped it away with the back of his hand. 'What do you write about?' He emptied his wineglass in one swallow. 'More wine, Prune. Prune! For heaven's sake, pay attention!'

Prune's face was a credit to his name. He sniffed disapprovingly as he filled Crispin's glass.

'Well...' Mary began uncertainly, poking at her dinner. 'I'm -'

Stanley held up his goblet. 'More wine here too, Prune. Get a move on, man!'

Uncorking another bottle with a small pop, Prune shuffled into second gear.

'I'm writing about a wildcat.'

There was a short silence.

'Excuse me?' the Heron wrinkled her nose with distaste as she turned to stare at Mary with open disbelief. 'You're writing about a...cat? Who on earth would want to read about a cat?'

Mary stared at her food. Aunt Maud looked up from savaging her plateful of venison and smirked behind her moustache. 'Dear Mary is writing about a particular cat ~ that one.' She pointed with her loaded fork to where I was quietly stalking across the floor in pursuit of my own dinner.

Heads turned to stare rudely. Mustering my most aloof expression I stared back, eyes smouldering. They returned to their conversation and I to the hunt.

'Children love animals,' Mary quietly explained, a defensive note creeping into her voice. 'So why not write a story from a cat's point of view? I'm hoping to...'

Intent on her stolen apple, the old rat hadn't heard my feather-soft approach. The loud chatter of conversation, Prune's wheezing and the clatter of salvers and silver drowned everything out. I approached slowly on her blind side. Her milky orb gave no warning, but the rat's instinct and her whiskers saved her at the last. As I wiggled down and bunched my muscles, she detected a shift in the air and shot out from beneath the walnut dresser and under the dining table. Only Prune observed her flight and my more sedate pursuit. The little man's eyes popped. He opened his mouth then shut it, and opened it again but the words stuck in his throat. The only thing in danger of coming out were his false teeth.

'Do you really think so?' Crispin was saying in a patronising tone to Mary. 'Well I never! Prune?' Looking up he clicked his fingers imperiously at the butler. 'More gravy here. Don't just stand there gawping, man! You look like a goldfish.'

Prune closed his mouth with an audible click. His eyes flickered towards me and then briefly back to Crispin. As I slipped beneath the tablecloth I swear a faint smile tickled his whiskered lips.

'Good grief, step-aunt,' Crispin complained loudly, as Prune hobbled round the long oak table as fast as his arthritis would allow. 'At least McFie didn't take all day about it, even if he didn't know his proper place. If I were you I'd sack this chap and hire a decent butl - arrrrrrrrgh!'

But his cry was drowned out by a horrendous shriek, as the dining table erupted into chaos.

Taking refuge beneath Aunt Maud's voluminous skirts, the old rat had thought herself safe. I pounced. As her skirts took on a life of their own, Aunt Maud let rip a scream of outrage and aimed a vicious kick at me. She hadn't even seen the rat! I yowled and Mary leapt angrily to her feet. Weaving deftly around chairs and legs, the cunning old creature scrabbled up a long pair of stockings and out of my reach. I shot out beneath the chair. The Heron shrieked hysterically as the equally agitated rat ploughed through her dinner, leaving little gravy paw prints on the pristine tablecloth. Her wineglass shattered on the table splattering wine over Stanley. Caught by a wildly flailing fork, her necklaces broke. Pearls rattled to the floor like hailstones as the Heron fled from the dining room, but all eyes remained riveted on the drama being played out on the table.

As Prune stood rooted to the spot, the rat ploughed gamely on through a dish of potatoes. Tripping over the salt cellar she knocked over a candelabra. Unable to stop, she pirouetted gracefully through Crispin's loaded plate and landed in his lap along with most of his meal. There was a loud crash as both chair and man fell backwards. His heavy kilt and sporran flew upward presenting the table with a matching set of tartan boxer shorts. With a cluck of consternation, Prune finally cranked into action, throwing a well-aimed napkin over the offending underwear, which merely fuelled Crispin's panic.

'Get it off! Get it off!' He was thrashing around dementedly on his back, stabbing down with a fork. Bits of fur flew in every direction. The rat however had already moved on and was making a break for it through the open dining-room doors. I let her go. This was far better sport. I pounced, and grabbing the object of Crispin's attentions, ripped it off and thoroughly savaged his sporran.

'Catastrophe!' Shocked but clearly amused, George leant down and picked me up and handed me to Mary who smothered her smile in my fur.

'Oh, get a grip, man,' George said unsympathetically to Crispin, who was still shouting in very unmanly fashion. 'The rat's long gone.'

He offered his arm to Mary's step-cousin, who was only belatedly realising the picture he was presenting. Beetroot red, he stood sheepishly, embarrassment rapidly turning to anger as he looked down on the wreckage of his Laird's outfit.

With a small puff of smoke, the smouldering tablecloth finally caught fire. Prune gleefully emptied a half bottle of vintage Chateau La Fitte over it. The entire room was a shambles. Mary and George began to laugh. Prune failed to smother a chuckle. At the head of the table, still on her feet, the Gargantuan One was positively puce with rage.

'That...animal of yours is nothing but trouble,' she snarled. 'It should be shot!' She brandished her knife threateningly at Mary who stepped back with me still in her arms.

'Now hang on a moment,' George turned angry eyes on his hostess who took a few steps backward and sat down hard. 'This whole performance was started by a rat; a muckle great thing. The castle is quite overrun with rodents. Catastrophe is doing you a favour by catching them. And by the way,' he paused to let his words sink in. 'It's illegal to shoot a wildcat, so I would make sure, if I were you, that His Grace doesn't go hunting, or he'll not just have the police and SSPCA to answer to, but me as well. Am I clearly understood?'

George was a big man and quietly determined. Aunt Maud swallowed her reply and subsided into her chair with all the grace of a Gloucestershire Old Spots pig in a sty.

'I shall have to go and change my kilt,' Crispin wailed. 'And look at the sporran!' he bent to retrieve it. 'The fur's quite ruined!'

'How very frightful, old chap.' George couldn't resist it. 'Dashed bad luck!' He caught the butler's eye. The faintest smile of grim satisfaction ghosted across Prune's face and was gone in a heartbeat. We had an ally!

'And anyway,' Mary warmed to a familiar argument. '*Real* men don't wear fur these days. You can buy perfectly good synthetic fur sporrans. You would never know the difference. There's no excuse for wearing real fur these days!'

To Dearest Edith

I padded through the silent darkened house. The doctor had come and gone, leaving the Heron sedated and thankfully silent. Eyes blinked on and off. Little claws skittered over the floor, escaping through ancient bolt holes in the skirting boards. I let them go, plump though they were. I was hunting two-legged animals tonight.

A still indignant Prune had already staggered off to the room he occupied near the kitchen and pantries. He had helped himself to several glasses of port on the way and was unlikely to wake again that night. If any of the family wanted anything they would have to fend for themselves!

Down in the silver pantry, I slipped beneath the floorboards and made my way to the forbidden west wing. I squeezed through the worn oak boards beneath the old dresser in the Trophy Room and kept to the deep shadows. A flow of cold air from the cellars made the reek bearable. Brogue shoes moved, barely inches in front of my nose.

'So, how many guests are attending our little ball?'

'I've the latest list from the Housekeeper.' The Gargantuan One spread out six pages of paper across the table.

'Three hundred and ninety-one.'

'So many?' the Duke purred fondly stroking his ridiculous moustache. 'You know, Maud, now Dreichandubh is ours there's really no need for this anymore, but...'

Old habits evidently died hard; they just couldn't resist the thrill of stealing from those they resented, of feeling they too were entitled to a life of wealth and extravagance. They were about to inherit a great estate; now they were hunting for sport, not out of necessity.

The Duke moved over to a large-scale map pinned to the wall.

'Righty ho, Maud. Operation Pumpkin it is! What's our modus operandi?' He took another slug of whisky. 'Where shall I start, do you think? Thistle Castle? What, what?' He tapped the map with his cane.

She nodded. He stuck in a drawing pin. 'Next?'

Lighting a cigar, Aunt Maud considered the sheets in front of her. 'Newbyth Hall and the Inversnekkies. They're always among the first to arrive. Make sure you get Lady Inversnekkie's sapphire necklace and – '

I confess I fell asleep for a while. Catnapping again, mind you... I was fully alert. By the time he threw another log on the fire, the map was ringed in a half dozen or so places, linked with coloured lines. They stood back and admired their handiwork. The Duke absently stroked his waxed moustache, adjusting its upturned wings to pointed perfection. What a strange place to have thick fur and an even stranger way to fashion it! Perhaps it is to attract a mate?

'Well, while you play the perfect hostess I shall net us a pretty haul. Easy as taking candy from a baby,' he crossed to the sideboard and topped up their glasses.

'To our business venture, Maud. To our wealthy neighbours; and of course, to dearest Edith, who made all this possible.'

'To dearest Edith!'

The Funeral

Nothing stirred. Even the corbies held their peace. A deep silence had settled over the glen and the frost-bitten moorland. The clear still night had chilled the castle's blue turrets and cloaked the woodlands in white hoarfrost.

While Mary prepared herself for the funeral, I sat and watched from a high window as the black cars, their polished carapaces glossy and hard as stag beetles, spilled mourners into the chill morning. Their footsteps left prints on the silver-blue gravel and frosted grass that crackled and fractured underfoot. The trickle of guests across the narrow stone bridge became a stream and then the stream became a flood that threatened to overflow the small chapel. Extra benches were dragged out of the summerhouse. Parked cars snaked far down the drive. Unlike her sister, Aunt Edith was evidently well loved. Many uninvited guests from the estate, who had come to pay their last respects, were left to stand outside.

Hidden from view by the soaring Scots pine trees, the chapel was a beautiful affair of soft red sandstone. Incense smoked and candles shivered. So did the family beneath their soot-black furs and feathers. They sang as sweetly as finches but sat hunched like raptors, eyeing their prey all the while, with mournful faces and dabbing tears that fooled no one save the priest. Only Mary had real tears to shed for all her feckless family. Squashed between the Gargantuan One and her husband, she wept silently, tended by his comforting arm.

Snow was falling in thick flurries by the time the priest turned from the graveside and the men, blue with cold, set their shovels to hard soil. The bagpipes keened a lament. Chalk white themselves, the mourners made their grateful way back into Driechandubh where Prune had hot coffee, tea and Cook's warming lentil soup to revive them.

A Highland Wake

With her aunt properly buried, Mary summoned up her courage to confront Aunt Maud. George was in the Library, hunting out material for his next book, so she decided to go on her own. I went along to lend my support. Aunt Maud was scared of me, so I reckoned that balanced the scales.

'But Aunt M - '

'No buts, my dear,' Aunt Maud held a theatrical hand to her bosom. 'Your dear Aunt, my dearest sister – may she rest in peace – insisted, yes *insisted* that we should press ahead. Sh – '

'But...' Mary was fired up. 'But how can we? How can we possibly have a Ball when Aunt Edith's just buried and the Will hasn't even been read. Until then, no one has the right to hold the Charity Ball in her stead. It should be cancelled or delayed!'

Aunt Maud's eyes narrowed. 'Oh, it should, should it? No, I think not! Following her instructions, the invitations were sent out over three months ago, and everyone who's anyone is coming. This is the social event of the year! As if we could just cancel this late in the day, when preparations are so advanced. No,' she flung her head back dramatically. 'We are holding a ball to celebrate dearest Edith's life and to raise money for her favourite charities. This will be a Highland Wake to remember! There is no more to say on the matter.' With that the Gargantuan One triumphantly returned to the menus.

I had no doubt that once the guests returned home to find their houses ransacked, it would indeed be a night to remember!

Campbell

We were on our way upstairs.

'Oh!' Mary suddenly stepped backwards. 'You startled me.'

Campbell was coming out of the Duke's guestroom. A strange play of emotions chased across the young man's pale earnest face. Fear followed by relief. He reeked of sudden sweat, though I doubt my mistress's petite nose could detect anything. So he, too, had something to hide.

'Hello, miss,' he smiled, confidently enough. 'A wee bit lost,' he admitted with an apologetic smile. 'I was looking for the guest laundry cupboard.' He held up a pile of sheets.

'Up another two floors, I'm afraid. Then turn to the right, third door on your left.' Mary smiled. 'It is rather a big house, isn't it?'

'As you say, miss.' Campbell's dove-blue eyes above his smile were watchful. 'Thanks. I'll be on my way, miss. Anything I can get for you, miss?'

'No thanks. And I'm Mary. Just plain Mary.'

'As you say, miss.'

'And you are?'

'Campbell, miss. Grandson of Mrs McFeeley; the sub-postmistress, miss,' he added, seeing Mary's questioning look. 'Been away from home in the army, miss. 'Wow!' He suddenly noticed me and his reserve fell away. 'Felix, felix sylvestris!'

Mary warmed instantly to his tone of admiration. 'You recognise him?'

'Aye, miss, I do that.' The young man held out his hand for me to inspect. He'd have to do better than that! Still, I deigned to sniff his fingers on passing. 'He's stunning! What happened?'

'We think he was shot by a keeper. We came on him by pure luck on the Inverarric road. He was in the vet's for two months, but he's pulled through and now all that shows is a slight limp.'

'Aye, I see it. The left flank?'

Mary nodded. 'Lots of metal pins. Major surgery. It's going to be a little stiff for the rest of his life.'

Campbell whistled. 'Never seen one domesticated before.'

'He's not really. Not like an ordinary moggie is. He's free to choose, to come and go. It wasn't easy.' She knelt down and held out her hand. 'Catastrophe, come here, puss.'

'Catastrophe?' Campbell smiled, intrigued at the name. It suited me well, I thought, for a name given by a furless-one.

'Well,' Mary smiled. 'We're going out for an evening stroll. You can only take so much of Aunt Maud. Goodbye for now.'

The Polis

'It's the polis, Ma'am.'

Aunt Maud looked up irritably from her guest list with a question mark on her face. 'The *what?*'

There was a crash from the fireplace. Aunt Maud looked round irritably to where the Duke was picking himself up. A tumbled brass scuttle had scattered its contents over the rug. A maid was just rising from setting the fire.

'Beg pardon, Your Grace,' the maid stuttered, her cheeks red with embarrassment.

Turning back to Campbell, Aunt Maud repeated herself. 'The what?'

'The p - '

'Stupid, glaikit girl,' the Duke took a swipe at the maid. 'Leaving a coal scuttle there where someone could trip over it.'

'But you weren't look - '

'You should be sacked for tripping me up. In my day in the ar–'

'But...'

'Douglas!' the Gargantuan One warned. There was a hard edge to her voice. She turned back to the footman. 'You were saying?'

'The polis, Ma'am,' Campbell repeated patiently. 'An Inspector Morrell.'

To do her credit she rallied admirably and the bright sunlight hid her mushroom-pale face from close scrutiny.

'The po-lice! Good grief, man, can't you speak English properly? Police! Well, show Inspector Morrell up immediately.'

They couldn't resist a quick glance there and then, the briefest of hidden messages. The Duke stretched. 'No need for me to stay, Maud, is there? I'll leave you to it, then. One or two things to see to...'

But he'd left it too late.

'Mrs McGregor. Why, Your Grace, good morning.' The man, in his early fifties, held his tweed deerstalker in his hands, a polished wooden pipe in his teeth and a regretful expression on his long affable face as he stood in the door. He sidled apologetically into the room.

'Dearest lady. May I offer my condolences and my apologies for disturbing you at such a time?' Sandy hair dusted with grey fell over his amber-brown eyes, fringing his face like a highland bull. Taking three steps into the room he gazed openly around with childlike interest, gawking at the huge painting over the fireplace; looking at the tapestries that hung on the whitewashed walls; the splendid Chippendale chairs and costly chintz fabrics that fell in folds around the arched windows. Why, then, did I sense that a fellow hunter had entered the room?

'My apologies, Ma'am,' he repeated, advancing on Aunt Maud.

'Pardon?' So she was flustered...

The Inspector frowned. 'On your sad bereavement, of course, Mrs McGregor,' he waved his pipe in the air. 'Lady Edith is a great loss to the estate and to the village. Indeed to the entire community of Braeside. Your sister was much loved, indeed if I may be so bold, I counted her as a personal friend. When my great aunt fell and broke her hip, your dear sister paid for her to be flown direct to Edinburgh itself to a private hospital - '

'Oh yes, yes,' the Gargantuan One recovered admirably, plucking her lacy handkerchief into service again, dabbing her eyes before blowing her nose loudly. 'Sniff. So like dearest Edith. Sniff.' She was stalling for time. Trying to work out why he was here. He didn't give her that time.

'May I?' The Inspector sat anyway without waiting for an answer and offered her his rumpled handkerchief. Her mouth twisted with distaste but her own was, on the evidence of our ears, quite exhausted.

'Mrs McGregor,' he leant forward pressing his handkerchief into her hand. 'Please forgive my intrusion at such a delicate time...'

'Yes, yes, very sad,' the bereaved lady blinked through her tears as she leant away from him. Now she was even more flustered. The inspector's voice was so soft she wasn't sure what he said next. My hearing is keener than the furless-ones'. 'But,' he continued. 'There have been a number of thefts...'

73

'Pardon?' That made her sit up. 'Thefts?' she quavered, an expression of polite confusion settling on her bovine features. 'Oh! How absolutely dreadful. Dooo tell us more, Inspector Morsel.'

'Morrell,' he corrected her.

Curled on the back of the sofa, I saw Campbell stop for a split second before smoothly straightening. Having set the fire, he left the room unnoticed, as good servants should. But I heard his soft footsteps out in the hall as he footered about adjusting a pot-plant, all the while listening.

'I don't understand, Inspector Morsel. What thefts?' She too could play games.

'Morrell. There have been a number of unsolved thefts in Braeside over the last decade. You may have noticed the reports in the local papers?'

'Ah yes, I think indeed that, yes, I may have noticed, but with dearest Edith requiring so much care, one just ignored it.... But why on earth, Inspector, should that worry us now?'

'We think that they may have been carried out by the same gang who are getting bolder. Only just last week, Colonel Blair reported a break in at the Mallory Hall. His butler had to be airlifted to Inverness Hospital with head injuries.' He was watching her closely behind that long fringe.

'Oh!' There was no mistaking her genuine shock this time. The Duke stiffened ever so slightly, but the Inspector was not looking at him, instead he reached forward to pat Aunt Maud's arm. '*Dear* Lady, I hope I haven't alarmed you...? I just thought that, given how vulnerable you must be feeling right now, the gang might take advantage of your plight, of the disruption caused by the recent funeral and so on...' he trailed off. 'The Hallowe'en Charity Ball.'

Behind them, the Duke made his excuses and softly walked out. I heard him quietly running down the stairs and along a landing before his footsteps faded. Campbell's followed more slowly.

'Oh, Inspector,' Aunt Maud warbled, inching along the sofa to cut off any escape. The Inspector would have to push her aside to get up now. 'So *very* kind of you to think of us.' Her confidence had

74

returned, now that the immediate danger was clearly over and the Duke had escaped to cover their tracks. Overwhelmed by acres of quivering bosom, the Inspector in turn shifted away ever so slightly into the upright back of the sofa.

'Not at all, Ma'am,' his alert eyes had barely flickered at the Duke's silent departure, but he had noted it. 'All part of our job. You see, over the past ten years there has been a catalogue of thefts across Argyle and Sutherland and I am particularly concerned for you.'

'For me?' Aunt Maud fluttered her eyelashes at him with polite confusion. She certainly had backbone... and better glue.

'Well, it might be that Driechandubh is next on the thieves' list.'

'Oh, how dreadful! But whai should you think that, Inspector?'

'Well,' he began. 'It's rather strange.' He scratched his head to emphasise his confusion. A spark of hot ash spilt from his pipe onto his head. A curl of smoke wreathed upwards as his hair kindled. 'Is it not the case that this is one of the few major residences in Braeside that has escaped the thieves' attentions? It, may be, dear lady,' he continued, while vigorously patting down his hair, 'that you have escaped their attention because your security is better and your staff more vigilant. 'Oh,' she now leaned forward to touch his arm; neither of them had thought of that. 'How *dreadful*, Inspector Morsel. How *frightful*! What can one do?'

Backbone digging into the sofa's unyielding arm, the Inspector manfully waved his pipe around just to give himself some breathing space. 'I would like to send PC Woodey round to stay. Just to ensure your safety, until such time as things have settled down and arrangements have been made for the inheritance. Doubtless after that, the matter of improving security can be raised with the...main beneficiary of the Will, whoever that might be.'

'PC Woodey?' Aunt Maud's question was tinged with a faint note of alarm. That would crimp their nocturnal activities. 'I don't think I'm acquainted with him?'

'He's a young lad, Ma'am. Grandson of PC Williams. Only been with the constabulary four months. But keen as mustard!'

A look of satisfaction flashed across her face. An inexperienced boy would pose no threat to their plans. 'Why, Inspector,' she smiled generously. 'So very kind of you to think of a vulnerable old lady. I'm of such a nervous disposition that the presence of a policeman would be a great comfort. I'm so...' she racked her brain for a suitable description that was credible. 'I'm so very fragile at this desperately unhappy time: I can't eat, I can't sleep, I'm quite worn out with worry and distress. PC Woodey sounds an excellent young man and I shall sleep safer for knowing that he is to hand should any... burglars... come visiting. But pray, he must be discreet; I would not want those guests staying on for the Hallowe'en Ball to be further disturbed.'

'Dear me no, Madam,' the policeman exclaimed. 'I fully understand. He shall be the height of discretion itself. I know that this is a difficult time to enquire, but have you seen anything unusual? Anybody unusual on the estate, hanging around?'

'So hard to say, Inspector Morsel. One doesn't pay much attention to servants.'

'Morrell.'

'But I shall be sure to let you know.'

'I would like to brief your staff, Mrs McGregor. With your permission?'

Oh, she liked the sound of that. 'Your' staff. She rang the bell pull. Five minutes later Prune arrived, wheezing through his long hairy nose, his arthritic knees cracking a tune.

'Prune. Inspector Morsel is going to brief the staff. See to it.'

'Very good, Ma'am.'

They looked up as the Duke returned. He was his normal suave self. 'Why, Inspector,' he smiled brightly. 'You're still here?'

Inspector Morsel

Fortified and assisted by three scones with clotted cream, all washed down with a 'wee sensation', the Inspector had briefed the staff and introduced young PC Woodey, who was making an inspection of the property. He'd probably not be seen again for days. Conversation had turned to the old lady.

'Why 'tis a fine cup of tea you're making now, Mrs Anderson.' The Inspector returned his cup to its saucer before helping himself to a fourth scone and a generous spoonful of bramble jelly. Cook scowled with pleasure.

'Camomile, Mr Prune?' Cook reached for the jars of herbal teas as the butler came in. 'All from our own walled garden,' she explained to the Inspector. 'Lady Edith kept a fine garden.'

'Aye,' the Inspector said almost to himself. 'It's a sad day. She was a grand old lady.' He hushed his voice. 'What's to be happening to the castle? By way of the inheritance?'

'I'm sure I don't know, Inspector,' Prune clicked his teeth in disapproval. 'Nought to do with us small folk.'

Cook waited till the butler had left. 'There's a lot of talk,' she confided. 'What with old Grandpa McFie being dismissed by Mrs McGregor, and others besides. She is behaving as if the castle is already hers; 'tis not her place to be dismissing folk, yet what could be done? We all rely on the estate for a living. Foresters and gardeners, gillies and game keepers, shepherds...'

'Dismissed?'

'Aye. The chock was too much. Mrs McGregor telling Mr McFie he wasn't needed any more, and then Herself dying. Wasn't needed? 'Tis a sad thing not to be needed. Took the heart right out of him. He's to be buried this afternoon.'

'Aye', the Inspector nodded sadly.

'He'd never shirked a day's work in his life,' Cook was getting into her stride. 'The Black Watch and then head ghillie and finally butler to Herself. Grandma McFie said he wouldn'y eat.'

They shook their heads.

'Nor take a dram.'

'He stopped drinking?' The Inspector was shocked.

Cook nodded. 'Aye. When he stopped trinking, Katriona knew she was losing him then. When a man won't take a dram, ye know it's the end.'

'Aye,' the Inspector sighed. 'It's all changed since we were bairns. Son followed father, daughter followed mother in time honoured tradition. Now we're finding we're not needed. I -'

'And these robberies, Inspector. Do you have any clues?' Prune had just shuffled back in and taken a seat. He was looking pale.

'Well...' the Inspector reluctantly admitted. 'We've nae clue. Time was, there was only the one every now and again, but each year the number's increased. 'Tis always the grand folk with the big houses and the most valuable possessions that can easily be sold on the black market; so it's clearly the same thieves. But nae patterns that we can see otherwise. I know it's there; I'm just no' seeing it.' He shook his head. 'The thefts amount to millions. Don't know what I'd be doing with all that money...'

'Well, it's the telefision,' Cook declared. 'That's chust what it is. And the talking pictures. That's what folk want money for.'

'Televisions aren't that expensive now, Mrs Anderson.'

'Ach', she clucked. 'No, Inspector, the advertisements, that's what it is. Turns folk into magpies wanting all sorts of useless things that they'd never had a need for before. Bright, pretty baubles with no use to them.'

'Young folk today. Always out gallivanting,' the butler chimed up, with a sniff of disapproval. There was evidently not much in life that met with Prune's approval.

'Aye,' the Inspector nodded. 'You're richt there, Mr Prune. Our Sean wanted an iPhone 6 for his birthday. Our Megan wanted a dance mat and a', the Inspector wrinkled his nose with the effort of recall. 'A ghd hair iron.'

'A what?'

'A hair iron.'

'And what', Cook frowned. 'Would they be doing with a hair iron when they don't even iron their clothes?'

'Wouldn't they burn their heads?' Mr Prune asked.

They had a third cup of tea while they pondered that perplexing question.

Rumour Has it the Estate is Going to be Sold

The wind was heavy with snow as George and Mary and the castle servants attended their second funeral in as many days. While the minister spoke warm words in a bitter wind, I explored the tiny graveyard with its weather tumbled gravestones. Generations of villagers had lived and died in service to Driechandubh, their moss-eaten names remembered here in granite and slate. And so Grandpa McFie was laid to rest beside them, and the Widow McFie turned tearful eyes towards the castle and the architect of her loss.

The congregation then crowded into the McFies' cottage for soup and sandwiches and a wee dram. It was a sober affair, made worse by the fear that they, too, might not be wanted before the year was out. If there were no work to be had in Driechandubh, the youngsters would leave for the cities, and the village would die.

There was a knocking at the door and a young girl burst in, her anxious eyes seeking out Cook.

'Grandma! Grandma! There's a loud man at the door!' she piped out in a high voice. Excusing herself to the Widow McFie, Cook bustled out, granddaughter in tow. Speculation had turned to the Reading of the Will when she returned.

'Why, Mrs Anderson,' Mary stepped forward. 'Whatever's wrong? Here, sit and catch your breath. Are you feeling unwell? You're very pale!'

And so Cook was, in a right flap and a flutter; with high spots of colour burning both cheeks, her kindly face creased with concern. 'It's…it's…the castle…' She crumpled into a chair, tears welling.

'The castle?'

Everyone instinctively turned to gaze northwards as if they could see through several feet of stone and curtained windows.

'A stranger was inquiring in the village chust this very moment, asking where the old castle was! An American he was…said he's of a mind to buy it…owns a distillery down in Perthshire…taught he'd fancy a castle for when he's visiting Scotland!' Cook finally came up for air. 'He says that Driechandubh is up for sale!'

'No!' Mary went pale.

'Aye!'

'But that can't be!' Mary's shock was mirrored on a dozen faces. 'Aunt Edith's barely buried. And the Will hasn't been read! That can't be…'

They looked towards the castle again, but I know it was Aunt Maud they were really seeing in their mind's eye.

'I'm sure,' the Gargantuan One smiled condescendingly at the mud splattered, anxious young lady standing in front of her, 'that I don't know what you're talking about, Mary, dear. You should know better than to listen to idle gossip. And look, you've trailed mud all the way up the stairs and onto the Persian rugs!'

Face burning like a spanked bottom, Mary looked at her guilty feet.

'But it was Cook! And she doesn't gossip.' That wasn't strictly true. 'The American was in the village.'

'Oh?' Aunt Maud's expression was cunning, her smile cruel. Cook's days at the castle were doubtless numbered. 'Doesn't she?'

'No,' Mary rushed to Cook's defence, her jaw set. 'She doesn't! And who was that visitor who was just here, then? The one who's just left? He was American, wasn't he? Down in the village they're saying he's going to buy the castle for a holiday home in the Highlands.'

We'd passed him as we came through the front door, so she could hardly deny he had been here. But the old baggage was cunning as a fox. She knew she couldn't deny it.

'Down in the village…?' Aunt Maud mimicked unkindly. 'Yes, he was here. It just so happens he represents the consortium of estate owners who are providing wild game for the Hallowe'en Ball, and who are also donating towards Edith's charities. We were just discussing some of the arrangements. Would you care,' she asked, not attempting to hide her disdain, 'to see the lists?' She waved at an untidy scatter of papers on the desk.

'No,' Mary said in a small voice. She couldn't hear the lie in her aunt's words. 'No, that won't be necessary. I'm… I'm sorry, Aunt Maud.'

Goodbye to Cobwebs

The west wing was slumbering on, dreaming of past glories when the rest of the castle burst into a frenzy of activity. In long neglected public rooms, shutters were turned back and twelve-pane windows thrown open. Grates were cleared of soot and feathers and fires were lit to banish the creeping damp. Mirrors positioned just so to catch the light were burnished to brilliance. In the Great Hall unfamiliar breezes stirred the faded banners, rippled mildewed tapestries, and swept cobwebs and their architects from their foosty neuks and crannies.

Aunt Maud spent an entire morning discussing the menu with Cook. And the entire afternoon with Prune deciding upon which wines and champagne should be brought up from the cellars and how many boxes of cheaper wine should be ordered from wine merchants in Edinburgh for those with a less discerning palate. In the evening, she and the Housekeeper agonised over seating plans and which rooms were to be prepared for which guests, since many were coming a good distance and would naturally expect to be waited on hand and foot when they arrived.

The Housekeeper buzzed hither and thither, briskly directing multitudes of workers. The entire village, it seemed, took up residence in the servants' quarters of the castle prior to the Ball, but its stately halls and magnificent rooms absorbed them effortlessly, with barely a hint on the surface to suggest so many laboured behind the walls and windows.

Doors and windows were thrown open, allowing the frigid air to invade the dozens of bedrooms, bathrooms and parlours being prepared for guests. Pillows were plumped, linen sheets starched and blankets and eiderdowns fetched in their dozens from the airing cupboards. Tapestries were beaten, rugs were hoovered and windows washed. Then the first guests began arriving.

Costumes arrived and were unpacked. Valets and maids laid out the family's velvet and silk, satin and sequins and ironed out imaginary creases. The family preened in their custom-made hand-stitched costumes and Aunt Maud's maid had a wretched time of it letting out the seams of her mistress's costume a half dozen times, even though she had had the temerity to suggest that in the first place!

Downstairs in the silver pantry, Prune was supervising the counting out of knives and forks and spoons; in the port cellar, Prune was decanting port as old as he was; in the ice house, Prune was supervising the carving of ice sculptures; in the wine cellar, Prune was directing the selection and uncorking of wines; in the servants' quarters, a quietly hiccupping Prune staggered off to bed for a lie down.

And in the background, peering through a rhododendron bush or chilling the red wine or burning one of Aunt Maud's silk blouses with the iron, was PC Woodey, taking his disguise as a servant to heart, whilst watching out for unusual and suspicious behaviour. An alarmed guest reported his suspicious behaviour to the police.

Gradually, as the hours turned into days, the jarring discord of Downstairs and Upstairs came together in a single orchestrated harmony. In the Great Hall, acres of snowy damask tablecloths floated down to hide polished wood, only to disappear in turn beneath sparkling silver and tinkling crystal. Fountains of pale pink roses and ivy cascaded down in contrived disarray; burnished candlesticks groaned beneath the weight of tapered candles; and all in turn were surrounded by ranks of stiff, brocade- backed chairs. The army of helpers slowly subsided below stairs and eventually flowed back down the drive to the village to iron their uniforms and prepare for tomorrow's exhausting evening.

There were a thousand and one things to do if one's Ball was to be a social success and Aunt Maud most certainly wanted to throw the most memorable Hallowe'en Charity Ball in recent memory – a fitting memorial to her dear sister Edith, of course. Having moved Upstairs, the Gargantuan One was quite determined to stay there, and this Ball was her introduction to high society.

The Port Cellar

The kitchen was warm and full of delectable smells. Meats roasted and salmon poached in clouds of steam. Jewel-like jellies studded the dresser. Cook was crafting spun-sugar confections for desert. The pantries were filling up with tasty morsels. I watched the comings and goings with interest.

'Heather, child, down there please, thank you.'

'Ah, Mr Duncan, cheeses in the front pantry, if you please. Jock, give Mr Duncan a hand now. Och, Heather, did your mam not teach you how to pluck a pheasant now? It'll be after Christmas before you'll be finishing that...'

I lay curled next to the stove. Mary was lending a hand and was hard at work beating egg whites for something called 'pavlovas.'

'You're looking bonny, Mary', Cook tasted the soup and added a little salt. 'Marriage suits you.'

Mary coloured faintly with pleasure.

The sound of children's thundering feet crashing overhead made the copper pans clatter and sway.

'Ach,' Cook smiled fondly, as she dusted off her apron in clouds of flour. 'Listen to the wee angels. They're chust having a grand wee time.'

By the sound of it, the wee angels were getting closer. Then I started back in reaction to a rapid displacement of air. A small freckled boy skidded to a halt bare inches from where I had been standing a whisker before. Putting a finger to his mouth, he dived under the table. He had two red balloons bobbing in his wake. I retreated to the security of the range.

'And who's it you're hiding from, Jamie Cochrane?'

The boy stuck his cheerful head up as clouds of flour dusted him like snow. 'Rosemary, of course!' he grinned, grubby and gap-toothed. The balloons squealed against the grainy wooden table-leg. 'Don't tell her whe - '

Bang!

Shrieks and laughter.

Cook dropped her rolling pin.

Bang!

'Heaven's above', she cried. 'What a fright you gave me, laddie...'

'Catastrophe!' Mary was on her feet but not fast enough.

Barely had my ears heard the sound when my legs were racing to keep up with my heart. My claws scrabbled over stone flagstones as I shot under the table and through the nearest open door.

'Catastrophe!'

I darted this way and that, not noticing nor caring where, my tail following my nose following my frantic paws. Open doors, a corridor, through the port cellar, down a hatch, leaping wooden steps and down into the dark bowels of the castle and safety.

'Catastrophe!' Mary's voice was faint but frantic. 'It's only a balloon!'

Hide.

Run.

Flee.

The pain in my flank was burning.

'Catastrophe!'

Mary's frantic calls faded, along with the daylight world. Stacked bottles, dusty with age, were tumbled by my flight, spilling outraged spiders to the floor. Cobwebs dressed me in clinging silver lace. Rats skittered and fled. When I finally stopped, I could hear nothing but the drumming of my heart and the bellowing cage of my ribs.

Catacombs

Catacombs: what better place for a cat to hide than down here in the stony darkness? At some point during my flight I had crossed from the roots of the castle into the heart of the mountain at its feet. Strangely, broad steps led down and down past niches where dusty bones lay shrouded in armour. The silence of my refuge had a depth to it, but I knew I was not entirely alone. Bats and rats shared tenancy of this subterranean world and high overhead I could hear faint footsteps as Prune slipped down to the wine cellar for a medicinal port. My paws rested on bone-cold stone and the dry space was so still that every movement of mine rippled through the air, bouncing back to paint a three-dimensional picture of the honeycombed warren of rock. Scents lay thickly as dust, old brittle bones cracked beneath my paws.

A distant familiar vibration tingled beneath my pads and thrummed through every hair on my body. I followed the downward passage to its source, an underground burn that passed through the honeycombed tunnels beneath the castle. The texture of the air changed. It roiled and eddied, small movements bounding and rebounding off the damp cave walls. And now enfolded in the layers of darkness and stone was the constant soft drip of water, echoing and re-echoing through the cavernous air.

Down and down I flowed like water, my paws following my nose, each whisker mapping the hidden contours of the caverns and remembering them. Fresh air ruffled my pelt. It led me through a narrow passage to a wide cavern where tiny motes of light danced and the caves took on dim-hued shape. High above, a ragged patch of dove-grey sky brought with it distant sounds and smells of the moorland. Hidden from daylight, plump pipistrelles lined the walls beneath like a living vine, the continuous leathery folding of their wings sounding like the crackling of frosted leaves.

Strange then, suddenly to find a boat resting on the ebony water. No rotting hulk devoured by damp and neglect and the tide of centuries, but oiled and tarred and freshly scrubbed. Paddles rested on the planks, along with a large torch. Strange, too, to find fresh footprints in the mud. I took a closer look. Every creature has a scent of its own as unique as fingerprints, and this one was known to me. The boat stank of cigar smoke, a whiff of diesel, moustache wax and dog. Coarse sacking behind rotting garden furniture hid the reason why. So, this was where they stored their ill-gotten gains.

There, There…

The low and narrow entrance to the caverns lay well-concealed behind boulder and bramble. I took a leisurely path home, hunting mouse and vole and rabbit. Thorny gorse bushes hid me while I sat on a boulder and watched as night's long shadow claimed the day. Marigold lights sprang in every window and across the glen. Cheerful voices called out in the lavender gloaming. People headed home for the night.

I slipped in through the pantry window and stopped to help myself to some poached salmon and a bowl of fish eggs before going further into the house. Padding upstairs and along the corridor, I could hear a tearful voice.

'Oh, George, I don't want to lose him. We should never have come.'

'Hush, darling, hush. I know how much you love him. We'll look for him at first light.'

I nudged the door open.

'There, there,' Mary cooed reassuringly as she plumped up the cushion. 'Poor thing', she gave me a hug that almost crushed me. 'He must have thought the balloons bursting were a gun shot. No wonder he bolted.'

George raked the fire till the sparks flew up out of sight and the warmth bathed me in its benevolent glow. I ate the tuna they brought me and drank the bowl of creamy milk to the last drop. I declined the little fish-shaped biscuits. I am not greedy.

Ghost Fences

'Hallowe'en,' Mary explained to Cook's six year old granddaughter as the child battled with a pumpkin, 'is a really old custom.'

'How old?' Rosemary poked me with the spoon.

'Oh, em,' Mary looked at me. I returned her gaze with feline indifference. 'It's err, very, very old.'

Rosemary solemnly considered this, somehow sensing she'd been short- changed. She took a stab at the pumpkin with a spoon. I got pips and pith full in the face.

'Why do we carve pumpkins?' she asked as Mary picked gooey bits from my coat and out of my ears.

'Ah, well, pumpkins represent, err, well...' Mary considered. 'Once upon a time, the Celtic tribes, who lived in Britain before the Romans came, took the heads of their enemies in battle as trophies. Then, when the harvest was in and winter was coming, they would set those skulls around the clan forts to protect them from evil spirits. And they would light candles and set them in the skulls. We call that traditional time Hallowe'en.'

'Gosh!'

'They called them ghost fences. And we still do the same thing today, only we use hollowed out pumpkins carved with faces. And we place the pumpkins at windows and doors to protect our houses. Real skulls wouldn't go down very well.'

'Why not?' Rosemary asked, with the ghoulish interest of the very young.

'Emm, well, today we don't cut off the heads of our enemies. It's not a very nice thing to do.'

'Why not?'

'Umm...'

I left Mary to it and went downstairs to see what Rosemary's grandmother had to offer. It was sure to be better than being poked by pumpkin covered fingers.

The Hallowe'en Ball

The Gargantuan One looked like an approaching storm front. As she billowed up the corridor in black and sprinkled stardust, the apples bounced off the sideboard dish and down the stairs in their haste to get away. Her heavy tread was sufficient to put even the grandmother clock off its stride.

'Tut,' Prune clicked his teeth as he reached up to reset the pendulum.

Mary was the bonniest witch you'll ever see. She was belted in black beads that gathered in the simple woollen dress at her waist. It was the same dress she had worn to both Aunt Edith's and Mr McFie's funerals. She and George had no money for extravagant outfits.

Tapers were touched to chandelier and candelabra and night was rolled back. Bodhran, fiddle and pipes began their unruly songs. As the pipes took up, I threw back my head and joined in.

'Stop your caterwauling, you little fleabag,' the Gargantuan One hissed, as she bustled past. 'Vile, flea-bitten fur-ball.'

Ribbons of music floated out through doors and windows to settle on the glen like a magical frost. The moon cast its soft light; turning roads into pale scars that criss-crossed pools of deeper darkness.

Guests began arriving in ones and twos and threes, bringing brilliant colour with them from out of the dark night. Sugar-spun faeries with glittering fingers and diaphanous gowns beaded with pearls emerged from the night, alongside pale phantoms, ghosties and bogles; dark cloaked witches and wizards with fantastical hats and staffs swept in. A man masked as a unicorn with a long mane of ivory hair excited great attention, not least because, in my fright, I bit him.

Besides gold and diamonds, Aunt Maud clearly liked nothing better than to hear the sound of her own voice. Waddling forwards to greet her guests, she evidently felt the role of Lady of the Manor sat well on her ample shoulders. The huge witch's hat certainly sat well on her head.

A photographer had been hired for the occasion, doubtless so she could be seen in the right magazines with all the right people.

'Good evening, Mrs Primrose. So lovely to see you...'

'Lady Nair. And how is your husband, pray?'

'Mr and Mrs Johnstone and Emile, dear. We have brought in some...'

'Colonel Gibson, *so* delighted you could grace our little soirée....'

'Dame Janet! Such an honour to meet someone from the theatre. Ai –' This to an elderly lady with cropped grey hair and lively blue eyes, who had brought a broom with her, along with a tall thin man who Aunt Maud had pointedly ignored.

'Is that Edith's niece, Mary?'

The Gargantuan One frowned. 'Whai yes, Dame, but wh -'

'So you are Mary.' Negotiating her way around the Gargantuan One, the elegant lady smiled, taking Mary's hands between her white-gloved ones. 'I'm so very glad to meet you finally. My name is Janet Pringle. I knew your aunt well, my dear. We were at St Andrew's University together. At one point Edith was considering a career in drama. She would have been a huge success. But she met Herbert and they took off for the States. There! You didn't know that now, did you? Many's the time, my dear, that she talked fondly of you. She loved you like her own child. If I were you, I'd prepare myself for a surprise.' She smiled at Mary's confusion. 'No,' she put a finger to her lips. 'I'll say no more. Let it be Edith's final gift to you! Brrr,' she shivered, 'I have never quite got used to the Highland chill. Champagne, my dear, that's the thing, and lots of thermal underwear!'

Bagpipes skirled. Conversation and dancers dipped and swelled, tartan lines and sets formed, broke up, and re-formed in a kaleidoscope of colour. The fiddle cast its spell. The bodhran beat out its rhythm, faster, faster...the ceilidh was in full swing.

'To Edith!' All around the Great Hall and the gardens, crystal flutes of strawberry champagne were raised. 'To Edith!'

Aunt Maud is Undone!

No one can better a cat's instinct and mine held true.

'A drink, my dear?' Aunt Maud had ambushed Mary while George was talking to a fellow academic. 'To toast your Aunt? Just the one? No, no I insist. I know you don't drink, but this can surely be an exception. I shall fetch you one now.'

Mary could hardly refuse. Slipping from her neck I threaded between partygoers and stole up the stairs. Stretching over the banisters, I looked down to the table where a hundred bottles of champagne had been uncorked and high fluted glasses bubbled with pale rose liquid.

'James – '

'Campbell, Ma'am.'

'Whatever. Kindly refill the glasses of the Earl of Kinloss and his wife.'

'And which ones would they be, Ma'am?'

Aunt Maud pointed them out by their hats. They were at the far end of the hall. Cloaked by her voluminous outfit and broad-rimmed hat, she furtively took out a twisted paper packet. Quickly tipping the contents into one of the glasses, she stirred it with a long fingernail before crumpling the packet into her corsets. Straightening up, her sharp eyes caught mine. She smiled. A triumphant savage smile as if to say, what could a flea-bitten fur-ball do? I'd show her.

As she turned away, I darted down the stairs and behind her. Ducking beneath sequinned black, I leapt. The gown that had cloaked her wickedness now cloaked me.

I'd honed my claws earlier that day on a particularly accommodating piece of furniture in Aunt Maud's room. There was a satisfying rending as material stretched beyond the bounds that nature intended gave way with a sigh of relief. The whalebone corset decided to follow suit.

Crystal shattered at her feet. Heads turned. The camera flashed. With a shriek of outrage, Aunt Maud gathered up her bosom and fled to the safety of her rooms.

With the departure of the wicked witch, the dumbstruck silence disintegrated into shocked laughter. Scandalised conversation resumed. They all assumed the costume-maker had stinted on her stitching. Laughter tinkled with crystal flutes. Kilt and plaid mingled with satin and silk as sets reformed for The Dashing White Sergeant.

'Catastrophe!?' Mary was all amused bafflement. I sat there all innocence. A few fallen stars lay forlornly around me and on my head. As I curled myself around her boots a number of people congratulated Mary upon her magnificent witch's cat, even if I was the wrong colour. I permitted them to stroke me. Campbell stepped forward with brush and dustpan and some cloths.

'Well,' he muttered out the corner of his mouth as he mopped up the spilt champagne. 'Catastrophe, what a clever chap you are. I take my hat off to you.'

An alliance was struck.

Curiosity Kills the Cat

The piper's pibroch curled up through the battlements and around the chimneys, challenging the distant hoot of a tawny owl. The gargoyles' pained expressions showed what they thought of it all.

A cat's natural curiosity, you might say, led me to it: a crowbar in the puddled water. Harmless in itself, but the gap in the crenelated battlements gave the game away. You could see from the scored and chipped stone that considerable effort had been applied to topple the gargoyle from its ancient roost to fall in front of the postern door where we had parked. Careless of them to leave the tools of their guilt behind, but of course they were confident that no one would suspect a thing. Who but rooks and cats would ever come up here? Why, cat burglars of course...

Hidden from me by steeply sloping gables, their voices drowned by the pipes, the Gargantuan One and her accomplice were hauling a few bags through a skylight and onto the roof.

'Edith's room has already been ransacked?'

'Yes, yes!' she nodded irritably, her mind already on returning to her role as hostess to Scotland's wealthy and famous. They turned back to the skylight.

They were cunning no doubt. So Driechandubh was to be robbed tonight along with other guests to divert the Inspector's suspicion!

They were upwind of me and I had grown careless. The solid stone battlement walkway gave away no hint of her approach as I inspected the evidence of their treachery. Aunt Maud's talons caught me without warning.

'Got you, you odious creature!' she cried triumphantly. Her breath rolled off yesterday's breakfast of kippers, still stuck in her teeth. Gobbets of saliva sprayed over me. I hissed and spat back but her gloves were fashioned from heavy leather and she had the advantage of surprise. She moved swiftly to where the Duke was dropping strings of pearls and gold and diamond broaches into an empty toolbox. That done, he replaced spanners and hammers and screwdrivers on top. His little dog yapped and leapt with slobbering delight, trying to catch my tail.

'Right, that's your sister's jewellery,' the Duke looked up. 'What are you going to do with it?' He was dressed in wizard's black, a cloak and pointy hat. The Gargantuan One had changed from her witch's outfit into a large smock of black sewn with black beads. The effect was the same. She didn't need the pointed hat or the broom. And now she had her cat.

'We can't have this little bag of fleas leading anyone up here. The police are bound to search the house for evidence of the burglary.' Her gloating smile evolved into pure malice. 'Give me one of your bags quickly!'

She dropped me in, then swung me out over the edge of the building before releasing me into the night, no doubt hoping I would drown in the moat far below or be crushed on one of the gleaming cars scattered like petals on the gravel.

Foolish woman!

I ripped the tumbling bag with strength born of desperation. The air sighed as it parted to grant me passage. Stars wheeled across the domed dark sky. Lights and gravel and laughter spun. Her aim was off. I kissed a gargoyle's hunched wings before somersaulting onto a second's snout. Who would have thought gargoyles could prove such allies? Then the great conifers standing like sentries around the house rushed up to greet me in a resinous embrace that checked the speed of my fall. In a flurry of pine needles I fell to the ground. My momentum carried me into the moat where some adventurous younger partygoers had already jumped in, evidently not put off by the cold. My unannounced arrival caused some momentary consternation and shouts of disbelief, before they fished me out.

Totally drenched, I shook the cold clinging water from my fur and stalked away with as much dignity as I could muster. Aunt Maud would have to try harder than that! Perhaps she didn't know that cats have nine lives.

Bags of Loot

It was still dark, but morning lent a rosy underglow to the freshening sky. Mirrored by the loch, a thousand pinpricks of marigold from the castle outshone the fading stars. I sat invisibly on a cairn of rocks at the edge of the loch and watched the comings and goings as I cleaned myself.

Guests began departing, furs and cloaks flung casually about their shoulders, their feet crunching loudly on the gravel. Faces flushed with dancing, lovers strolled hand-in-hand across the stone-arched bridge. A wine bottle shattered on stone as someone flushed with drink laughed. Chauffeurs were roused from their slumber. Cars departed down the drive in ones and twos, the growl of their engines fading with distance.

There was the sound of an approaching jeep from the woods to the west, but no lights. The engine cut, but I could still hear it as it bumped and rolled along the dirt track. Padding round the edge of the water and into the woods, I could see it black against the grey shades of dawn. There was the faintest noise as the driver cranked the hand brake, then the door swung open. I crept closer through rough grass and bracken to observe my prey. Tonight the driver was dressed for stealth in soft dark clothes and boots, all swathed by a long black cloak. No badges, belts or buckles to reflect dawn's thin light. A woollen hat was pulled down over his face with holes for eyes and mouth, but I already knew who he was and where he was going.

Dark he might be, but the Duke breathed as loudly as the cattle in the field, puffing and blowing as he unloaded the back of the jeep. Then he clumsily moved the heavy bags into the cairn of rocks that hid the cave's entrance. He got back into the Land Rover and rolled it silently down the track through the cover of woods and from there onto the drive. Then he was back, puffing and blowing like a winded deer. He gathered the sacks one by one and deposited them in the boat. He never saw me couried down on the planking, motionless and invisible between two bags of furs. As far as he knew, I was lying broken and unmissed beneath the castle walls.

We rowed through the dripping caves, the sounds rippling back and forwards. A lance of light caught us in a bar of bright white lights. The dipping oar fractured it into a thousand dancing shards.

'Right.'

The single word almost made me jump out of my skin. I flattened against the bottom of the boat and gathered my muscles for an attack. 'Here we are.' It took me a moment to realise he was talking to himself. He swung a leg over the prow as the boat grated on shingle. Taking the rope he moved into deeper darkness. He grunted, testing it. Satisfied, he splashed around pulling one bag after another, not bothering with the noise he made. Bats rustled restlessly in the air above as the sacks joined others stowed away at the back of the cave. Pleased with his efforts, the thief paused to admire his stolen wealth.

'Well done, old boy. Jolly well done, if I say so myself!' Starting suddenly, he flicked his wrist to look at his watch. 'Damn!' Hastily covering his loot with old potato sacks he leapt into the boat and fumbled for the oars. The unburdened boat skimmed the surface of the underground lake, paddles churning its placid surface. I watched him go before leaping from boulder to boulder in silent pursuit. I already knew where he was headed. A scrap of fading starlight glimmered high above in the roof of the cave, bringing with it the first scent of dawn. Throwing his dark cloak about his shoulders, the burglar swapped his mask for the wide-brimmed pointy hat. His costume was plain, nothing to pick out of a crowd, nothing to draw attention.

I followed him as he slipped into a crack in the face of the cave wall. It was pitch black but he evidently knew his way, for he never paused. The passageway rose steadily, sometimes levelling off, only to rise again. We came to steps. Turning on his torch he took them two at a time. They soon opened up into a wider space full of cobwebs and spiders and a ladder. Light spilled through cracks in the wood floor above us. He paused there, head cocked to one side, doubtless listening for Prune. Satisfied, he slipped through and into the port cellar where he grabbed a bottle, and then carried on upwards towards the ceilidh.

One more wizard joined the drunken throng.

We've Been Robbed!

It was eleven o'clock that morning.

We were half way through a bleary-eyed breakfast when a frightful screech rent the air. It was followed by a loud thump and several crashes, followed by a second higher scream.

'George, darling!' Wide eyed with concern, Mary thumped her husband on the back. He'd sprayed his cornflakes all over the table. Milk dripped down his chin. He put his hand up to forestall her. 'OK. OK,' he wheezed, eyes watering. 'F-f-food went down the wrong way.'

The sound of running feet recalled the cause.

'What on earth was that?' Startled they looked at each other.

'C'mon,' he urged his wife. 'Let's take a look.'

The rising babble of voices led a growing throng onto the first gallery of the main staircase where Aunt Maud was lying groaning on the floor. Or perhaps it was the floor groaning? It doubtless had the greater cause. She was being fanned by Prune who appeared on the edge of panic, and having got down on his knees was quite unable to rise. The Housekeeper, Campbell and two of the housemaids were also there ahead of us. The family either hadn't heard or didn't care. They were probably nursing hangovers.

'What is it, what's happened?'

'Perhaps she should be moved to her bedroom?' kind-hearted Mary ventured, always ready to take someone on trust, even a creature as odious as Aunt Maud.

There was a moment's polite silence as every head turned in

her direction.

'And how, Madam,' Prune dryly enquired, 'do you propose we do that?'

Colour flooded Mary's cheeks. 'Em, I wasn't, em, thinking.'

'As you say, Madam.' Prune was evidently back on firmer ground. He turned back to his employer who, seeing the moment slip away, was beginning to flutter her new set of eyelashes in dramatic fashion, punctuated with a well-timed groan or two.

'Theft!' She whispered. 'Edith's jewellery has gone!'

I heard her words clearly. Those of inferior hearing didn't and several unfortunates who leant down to listen were subjected to an alcoholic after-haze that made their eyes water. Then she saw me at Mary's feet and her eyes widened, this time in genuine shock.

'But...' she nearly gave herself away as people looked towards me, too. 'Theft!' She croaked, getting back on track. 'Oh, my poor heart!'

I don't think she was fooling anyone save herself and the maids and Campbell, who seemed all solicitation and concern, though even he drew the line at offering the kiss of life.

'Madam?' Campbell asked, as he helped her to sit up, a major achievement in itself without a crane. By the end of this little exercise they were puffing and blowing, the former due to exertion and the latter because she doubtless felt it in character for someone in shock.

'We've been robbed!' she wailed dramatically, making the circling bystanders step backwards with their ears ringing. Campbell was very slow on the uptake. On cue, he dutifully chimed up,

'Robbed, Madam? Whatever do you mean?'

She could have written his lines for him.

'My d-dear sister's bedroom. It's been ransacked. All her jewellery...it's all gone! I left strict instructions that her room was not be disturbed – to, sniff – to preserve dear Edith's memory, sniff, and I was just passing by...sniff'

There was a general stampede to Aunt Edith's room, where, shock, horror, it was in the exact same state as when I saw it last, the only difference being that Aunt Maud was no longer nesting in the middle of the wreckage. Clothes and empty jewellery boxes and papers were scattered tapsalteerie about the room. Abandoned by her audience, Aunt Maud had slowly struggled to her feet and followed.

'Why, yes, Ma'am, the room's been ransacked,' Campbell confirmed. 'I'll try and find PC Woodey.' PC Woodey was roused from sleep in the servants' quarters and hadn't heard a thing the previous evening.

'Ohhh!' Aunt Maud rebuked his rumpled arrival with ill-concealed pleasure. 'What a useless young man you are! We've been robbed right under your very nose!'

Everyone turned towards the red faced young man who was hurriedly tucking his pyjama top into his trousers and trying to flatten his sleep-rumpled hair. Throwing a hand dramatically against her brow, Aunt Maud promptly sagged to the floor again. The shock was too much for half the pictures on the corridor wall, which promptly followed suit. When the sound of breaking glass and picture frames had subsided, someone called the polis.

Inspector Morrell arrived in a remarkably short time, shaken and rattled by the bouncing he had received in his old car. Prune saw him into the Morning Room where Aunt Maud, flanked by Aunt Edith's anxious stepchildren, awaited his arrival. He took off his deerstalker. Prune whipped it away, followed by scarf and coat. Hand on forehead in eloquent despair, the Inspector picked his way delicately through a clutter of abandoned champagne bottles, balloons and streamers.

'Dearest Madam,' he offered apologetically as he came forward. 'Your footman reported a robbery.'

Aunt Maud was itching with impatience to recount her drama once again, but was thwarted by her status as bereaved. She frantically fluttered her eyelashes and ostentatiously sniffed, bringing the gentlemanly Morrell to the rescue with another of his indescribable handkerchiefs. That dried her tears up at least.

'Why, Inspector Morsel,' she fluttered. 'So good of you to come so quickly.'

'Dear Madam,' he cried. 'Did I not warn you this might happen? Did I not say that the alarm system was hopelessly outdated? Did I not leave -'

'Yes, yes,' she smiled to take the sting out of her impatient rebuke. 'But there has been no time, what with the reading of the Will the day after tomorrow, and the Ball to organise. As you can see...' She gestured at the maids still tidying the house. 'No time at all. And we thought that PC Woodey would protect us!' she added accusingly, as if it were entirely the hapless constable's fault. The unfortunate young man had thrown off his disguise and was energetically interviewing all the guests, taking down copious notes in his little notebook.

'Quite so, quite so,' the Inspector soothed Aunt Maud. 'Perhaps, if you are able, after so distressing a discovery, you might conduct me to the scene of the crime?'

Everyone returned to the scene of the crime so that Aunt Maud could take him through the little drama step-by-step. During this time, the Inspector got out a little black notebook and a pencil of his own, but when it came to listing what was missing Aunt Maud said she had no idea; a bare-faced lie, given that she was wearing a great deal of the 'stolen' jewellery about her considerable self.

'None at all, Madam?' he frowned. 'Perhaps there is was an inventory? For insurance purposes?'

'No,' she said, a little too quickly.

'No?' he echoed. 'No to which, Madam?'

'Pardon?'

'No, there is no inventory, or no you cannot recollect?'

Now she was a little flustered and took refuge in her fainting routine, so that he conducted her to a sturdy chair to allow her to recover and to think.

'No,' she said slyly sticking to her first effort. 'No, I really can't say what Edith kept in her room, except perhaps for a few particular pieces that she wore a great deal. I would have to look through her papers. Or perhaps her solicitor might know. He is in fact arriving tomorrow afternoon.'

If there were papers, there wouldn't be any by the time anyone else got there.

'Quite so, quite so, Madam.' the Inspector nodded sagely. 'Well, if you could, of course – as soon as you feel able – draw up any details whatsoever – a description…an estimate of their value? Anything at all that might help with our investigations? But since we are here, perhaps you could take a look around right now? I see there are many empty jewellery boxes, for example…?'

We left Aunt Maud and the Inspector to it.

Below stairs, George was apologising to Cook for the shambles that had been the breakfast table.

'Och, don't you be worrying now,' she patted his arm kindly. ' Twas a ghastly shock we were all having. She's a fine set of lungs on her has Mrs McGregor. We heard her in the kitchens.'

Mr Crankshaw

The sky was dove grey and webbed with clouds that promised further rain. A chilling wind blew out of the north, bringing with it skeins of geese that honked and chuckled their way south.

I was perched on a window-seat beside Mary. She and George were talking in lowered tones as they packed. The Will was to be read the next day, after which we would be immediately heading home. Whatever the Will revealed, Mary evidently didn't expect to profit by her aunt's death and she could not abide staying one day longer with the Gargantuan One ruling the roost.

A bouncing blue car covered in mud slowly made its way up the drive, as its driver tried to avoid each and every pothole. By the time it arrived, so had Aunt Maud. She swept in wearing a matching Pringle set of palest lavender that showed off every ripple, tuck and bulge. A Dior scarf was placed just so around her neck, reducing her number of chins to two.

'Our guest, my dears, has finally arrived.' She wrenched the bell pull to summon Campbell. Afternoon tea was duly ordered but had not arrived by the time we heard footsteps out in the hall. Prune knocked on the door with quavering hand to announce the visitor.

'Madam, Your Grace, Miss Mary, Master George...'

'Prune,' The Gargantuan One was all impatience. 'Doo get on with it.' Squashing her irritation beneath her gritted teeth, the Gargantuan One beckoned their hesitant visitor in.

'Mr Crankshaw,' she boomed. 'Doo come in, dear man, doo come in. Mary, George, dahlings, doo let me introduce an old family friend, Mr Edmond Crankshaw.'

Her *dear friend's* eyes opened wide at the introduction. Friend indeed!

Rake thin and stooped, the old gentleman wore a smart pinstriped charcoal suit and black tie. His short silver hair radiated out like thistledown. He, too, looked as if he would blow away in the slightest of breezes. He offered each a limp handshake in turn, but held Mary's a fraction longer. She glanced up at him in surprise, finding herself gazing into clear intelligent eyes and a gentle smile.

Campbell arrived with a salver set for afternoon tea. The finest silver tea-set was followed by a feast of sugar-spun pastries and crustless sandwiches, arranged just-so in three-tiered dishes. Cherry scones and profiteroles were heaped in pyramids. I was learning a lot down in the kitchens with Cook.

'No, no, Campbell,' the Gargantuan One waved the young man away. 'Ai shall serve maiself. Two sugars, Edmond?' Aunt Maud was jollity itself. 'And a dash of milk?'

'Thank you, but how do you kno - '

'And Mary, dahling, raspberry tea for you. No one can say I don't look after my niece. Scones? Shortbread?'

Mr Crankshaw settled himself down carefully, placing the large leather briefcase by his feet before taking up his flowery cup and saucer. Aunt Maud watched its every movement out of the corner of her eye.

'A sad day, Madam, Miss.' Like many others before him, Mr Crankshaw offered his sincere condolences to both women. Behind his moon spectacles, tears pricked. He nodded sadly. 'A sad day.' So the old man was genuinely fond of the old lady, too. Everyone loved Aunt Edith dearly, it seemed, except her envious sister and her grasping stepchildren.

'Well,' Aunt Maud smiled in robust good humour, as she bit into her third cake. 'Saddle of lamb for dinner tonight. I doo hope you have a good appetite, Edmond?'

Cat Burglar

Mr Crankshaw retired from dinner early, clutching a hot toddy and a hot water bottle. 'A l-l-ittle tired, Madam. Not so young as I used to be!'

Mary hid a smile behind her left hand as the gentleman said his goodnights, awkwardly kissing her right hand. 'You remind me of your aunt,' the old man turned at the door. 'A wonderful lady she was, too.'

Mary blushed at that. The Gargantuan One scowled.

'Ah well,' The Duke stretched theatrically. 'Yawn, yes well, yawn, I too must retire, Maud. A rather busy few weeks catching up with me.' The Gargantuan One smiled at that. A secretive inward smile.

'No, no, sit, no need to remember that I'm a Duke, really.' He clicked his heels and bowed his head briefly before retiring.

Cook had already gone to bed, and the kitchen was lit only by the dying glow of the range, when they entered. They didn't see me curled by the stove.

'Are you certain?' The Duke cursed as he collided loudly with a chair.

'Quiet!' she hissed. 'Of course I'm certain! He's an old fool well past retirement. A cup of warm milk will be just the thing to settle him down. If there was one thing I learnt about him on his previous visit a year ago, it was that he's regular as clockwork in his habits. Bed at ten. Cocoa at eleven.'

'But the quantity?' her companion persisted.

'How do I know?' She shrugged her massive shoulders as she broke open pill capsules and emptied their contents into the sugar bowl. 'They're sleeping pills aren't they? A half dozen should surely do the trick.'

'What if he notices?'

'It's white isn't it?' she snapped. 'Anyway, Prune is short sighted. No, no one is going to notice a thing. Getting cold feet, my dear? It's supposed to be easier the second time. After murdering Edith, this is child's play.' She laughed unpleasantly. 'Sweet dreams, old man.'

They carefully replaced the sugar bowl on the table. The pill bottle was pocketed. A bell sang out. They froze. Every eye, including mine, swivelled upwards to where three dozen pewter bells hung above the huge dresser. Frayed and yellowing cord disappeared through small holes in the soot-blackened ceiling. Below each bell a name was written in an elegant hand:

The Morning Room
The Billiards Room
The Lounge
The Blue Bedchamber
The Great Hall
The Library
The Armoury
The Music Room...

'That's him,' Aunt Maud hissed. 'Quick.' Tiptoeing, they slipped through the pantries and out by the garden door. They needn't have worried. The little bell had rung twice more before Prune arrived to gaze up at the vibrating bell. Blinking owlishly, he set about his task. In due course the tray was loaded with a jug of hot cocoa, sugar, cup and saucer. For good measure Prune added some chocolate biscuits. He rattled off down the pantry corridor, muttering and mumbling about the lateness of the hour.

'He's gone?'

'Yes.'

They tiptoed in again to inspect the table.

'Right. How long should I give him?'

She consulted her watch. 'Better leave it till midnight to be safe. I've put him in the Blue Bedchamber, so no need to worry about bumping into my niece and her beloved.'

'Good thinking,' the Duke nodded vigorous approval. His wig slipped slightly over his left ear. 'Right, I'd better go and get my things from the old study.'

'You have the forged Will exactly like the other?'

'Of course!' he sounded offended.

Satisfied, they disappeared a final time into the gloom of the garden. If anyone asked, they would simply be taking a stroll. It was, after all, a wonderful late autumn evening.

The Witching Hour

It was well past the witching hour but my hunch paid off. As you doubtless know, cats can wait absolutely motionless for long hours, waiting for the right moment to strike. I couried down in the hall under a dresser. The grandfather clock had barely struck one o'clock when a door down the passage slowly opened. Aunt Maud must have oiled the hinges because it never made a sound. Soft footsteps came up the corridor.

Dressed in shades of grey, the Duke crept down the moonlit corridor, keeping to the shadows. He moved with a natural stealth and confidence that suggested he had done this before, many times. For a two-legs he was good, very good. I was better. He had a small bag slung over his back. I followed. Along and up the servants' stairs, he then tiptoed along the carpeted hallway to where the lawyer was accommodated. He paused briefly at the door, head cocked to one side, listening. I could hear the snores from where I was. Similarly satisfied, he stole into the room. So... the Duke fancied himself as a cat burglar did he? Well, we would see about that.

The Secret Study

The clock had barely chimed the quarter hour before they were back in their den. I was hardly there before them, when a section of bookcase swung silently open and the two conspirators entered. So that was their secret entrance! How they moved throughout the great house without being spotted. I resolved to take a midnight prowl of my own in due course, to explore these hidden trails.

Shrugging off a dark jumper, the Duke moved across to the fire and threw a thick wedge of papers into the dying fire where they smouldered fitfully.

'Righty ho!' he was in a jovial mood. 'That's the last anyone will see of Edith's true Will. As of this moment, my dear, you are the heiress to Driechandubh!'

The Gargantuan One grunted sourly. I could smell her tension. She lit a cigar and sank back into a sagging armchair. The odour was quite foul. I coughed. She was immediately still. I could feel her suspicious predatory eyes raking the room. I froze a snarl on my face and my tail full-blown in a pose similar to the stuffed creatures around me. I didn't need to pretend I felt threatened. I had long since recognised an inveterate animal hater when I saw one. I doubted she was familiar enough with the animals to spot one living creature amongst so many dead ones, and her co-conspirator, who might have, wasn't even looking. Her eyes passed over me.

'It's only the wind, Maud,' the Duke chuckled indulgently. Polished court shoes strode over to the sideboard. Crystal clinked.

'Auchentoshan?'

She grunted her agreement, mean eyes still watchful.

'Relax,' he smiled as he poured the malt whisky. 'No one suspects a thing.' He handed her the drink.

'Slainte mhath, slainte mhor! To our little scheme.'

'To our little scheme.' She drank the amber liquid in one swallow of those massive jowls.

'I think,' she declared judiciously, 'that I can manage another. And, Douglas, dahling? Doo make it a large one this time. It's going to be a long day.'

He's Asleep!

The Morning Room was one of the smallest rooms in the old part of the castle. It was in the east wing, looking south over the loch towards the moors and the distant corries. This morning the sun reached out with warm fingers and drenched the world in butter- yellow, but even that failed to melt the frozen heart of the loch, and doubtless failed to thaw the hearts of the guests who crammed into the tiny room before the clock struck ten. They shuffled and glared and fought for positions like carrion over a kill.

Aunt Maud was camped out like a tent, in the front row strictly reserved for family. Unfortunately, with her there no one else could fit except

Crispin and Nigel. Behind her, the Duke mopped his brow with a monogrammed handkerchief. The room was freezing.

Tick, tock. Tick, tock. The clock on the desk continued its endless measuring of time. The mourners began to shuffle and cough. There was a whispered exchange between Aunt Maud and the Duke. Watches were consulted. Aunt Maud and the Duke had another exchange. Aunt Maud smiled a sickly smile, designed to instil confidence. She rang the bell pull. Prune was duly despatched. The Gargantuan One and the Duke hovered anxiously in the hall. Unable to contain herself, Aunt Maud bustled off. The clock chimed the half-hour. We could hear her weighty footsteps returning.

'The old man's fallen asleep!' You could clearly hear her in the perfect silence. 'He can't be woken.' Aware that they were talking too loudly they dropped their voices. There was a muttered conference that became heated.

Whisper... 'doctor'.... 'No!'...whisper...

Every ear in the room save mine was straining to listen as they bickered. Aunt Maud came in clasping her hands. For once she looked shaken.

'Mr Crankshaw is, err, indisposed. Yes, indeed, indisposed. He is not feeling well... at all. No. Not at all well. I am sure that after a short rest he will be able to continue. In the meantime we are preparing a light luncheon.'

'Don't you think', Mary stood. 'We should call for Doctor Heggie?'

Aunt Maud turned cool eyes on her niece. 'No, no, not at all. Nothing to worry about,' she shook her head firmly. 'He's an old man, that's all. No need to call for a doctor. No, no need at all...' Aunt Maud shut her mouth determinedly 'And let that be an end of it!' She turned back to the guests. 'Luncheon will be served within the hour.'

Mary and her husband stared after the retreating hostess.

'What was that about?' George mused.

The short rest turned into an afternoon, and finally a day. Staff were run off their feet preparing guest rooms that had only just been stripped and aired after the Ball. Below stairs, Cook laboured to create something new with leftover dishes. Above stairs, Prune and Campbell laboured to keep the bickering family happy.

The following morning they descended again, determined to have satisfaction even if it meant dragging the old man out of his bed. Thankfully, the old man managed to get himself out of bed, although it was a near thing. He was all mumbled apologies at breakfast, but Aunt Maud was all care and concern, there was no task too small that she could not do for him. She had seen her plans nearly derailed and how close they had come to disaster; if he could not continue and another younger lawyer were to take his place, their deception might not work.

The Will

I have never seen an old man shake so. Glassy eyed, the lawyer swayed on more than one occasion, as if blown by a strong wind the rest of us couldn't feel. He took an eternity to unzip his leather case and bring out the envelope. He dropped the envelope twice and nearly slipped off his seat when a leg caught the edge of the rug. At this point, the Duke and The Gargantuan One could not resist a sideways glance at each other. The old man's every movement was economical and measured. The pair of them squirmed with impatience as if a colony of ants wriggled in their underwear.

There was a moment's consternation when Mr Crankshaw couldn't get the envelope open, and Prune was sent to the study for a letter-knife. The atmosphere wound tighter and tighter, stretching the very air. I could sense the storm was about to break.

'Well,' the lawyer looked up into a sea of faces, fixed with the frozen grin of a polar explorer, and faltered. 'Ll-a-dies and gentlemen, good morning...Apologies that..that you have been inconvenienced...'

Whether it was convention or simply his habit, he began with small bequests and grants.

'To Mr Anderson, Driechandubh village postman, a bequest of £400 to assist in the repair of his cottage roof. To Mrs MacDonald, postmistress, a pension of £600 a year. Mr Fawkes, ghillie, £1,000 for him and his good wife and the right of tenancy for life...Jenny Campbell and her husband, a Mediterranean cruise on the occasion of their golden wedding anniversary on 16th December and a portfolio of £5000 for their grandson, Bruce...'

Bored stiff, the family allowed themselves the occasional judicious nod as one servant or another was bequeathed a suitably small amount.

But...there were outraged hisses as Woolworth, the head ghillie, inherited the vintage Jaguar and Mrs Cumbernauld, the late Aunt's maid, the Cairngorm earrings and bracelet that Georgina had always so admired. Anxiety increased. The smell of the hunt flooded the room. Fingers began to tap; eyes began to cross with ill-concealed impatience. Watches were repeatedly consulted.

'To my niece's husband, George, I bequeath the Driechandubh Chronicles.'

That excited no comment among the vultures at all. They clearly were not interested in foosty old books and maps. George was ecstatic. Bouncing up and down on his seat like a child, his excitement lit up the gloomy gathering.

Aunt Edith clearly cared for those in service to her estate. It took two hours in total. After all that, Mr Crankshaw had to go and refresh himself with a sustaining cup of elderflower tea, leaving everyone in an agony of suspense.

Crispin smiled in triumph as the vintage Rolls and Aston Martin were left to him. Georgina preened like one of the peacocks on discovering she had inherited the villa in Tuscany. Nigel was getting very anxious indeed, before learning that the collection of Armada gold coins was his. A promising start, they doubtless thought, to what would, of course, be their rightful heritage.

'Ahem'. The lawyer cleared his throat. 'Furthermore, my dear step-son, Nigel, may keep the Ferrari he, ah... borrowed three years ago. To dear Georgina, I leave the square-cut emerald set in a gold ring that she remarked upon so often. And to Crispin, the estate shall write-off the debt of £40,000 owing on his failed business venture in Bognor Regis. To dear Herbert's children I also bequeath a single grant of one hundred thousand pounds each.

'What?' Crispin started to rise from his seat.

Aunt Maud alone neither squiggled nor squirmed nor sweated. Instead, a fey glint lit her eyes.

'The remainder of the e-e-state of D-D-Driechandubh, its paddocks, policies, the grange and l-l-logging business are left to..to tooooo.' He sounded like a baby owl practising.

Nigel and the Heron leapt to their feet in protest.

'But surely,' Nigel quivered with indignation. 'You've only just begun. What about the rest of Daddy's business interests.... The businesses...?'

'What!' the Heron cried at the same time. 'That can't be - '

Only Crispin retained his seat, looking unbearably smug. As the eldest, he doubtless felt it quite appropriate that he should inherit the lot.

The lawyer tried again. 'Toooo my d-d-dearest n-n-n-n...'

It was as if his mouth had begun something but his eyes were telling him different. He trailed into silence, staring at the paper as if it had just bitten him. He was the centre of attention now.

'T-t-to my dearest...nnnn' he tried again, frowning at the paper as if willing the words into submission, but he got just as stuck. 'Ladies and gentlemen, if you'd j-j-ust bear with me.' He beckoned Campbell forward and whispered instructions.

The entire audience leant forward as if blown by the wind.

There was an awkward five minutes before the young man presented him with a second slim leather bag. The lawyer unzipped it and rummaged through its contents. He brought out a sheaf of papers and laid them precisely beside the first. He turned one page then the other.

So he had brought more than one copy of the will! Several more minutes ticked by. Now his audience was becoming openly restive. Unable to contain herself, Aunt Maud strode forward, blotting out everyone's view. The solicitor quailed and called for Mary to join them...

Two chairs were brought forward and a whispered conference took place.

'D-dear ladies, I'm at a loss for words, but - '

'We can see that,' Aunt Maud snapped peevishly, looming over him like a cliff. 'Try, man, what's the problem?' Anxiety was making her bellicose.

'Well, you see, err, this will, err, isn't exactly the same as this one.'

Mary stared at the lawyer. 'I'm sorry,' she said. 'I haven't the faintest clue what you just said.'

'Yes, man, spit it out', the Duke had invited himself to their little conference. 'What the dickens is the problem?'

'Err, Your G-g-grace, err, the thing is, that err, well, I can't believe it, but, err, these err, two wills, well you see, the thing is that they're not the same.'

'You're havering man,' the Duke said unkindly. 'Let me see.'

Having finally got it out, the exhausted lawyer sagged into his chair. The family surged forwards and the room disintegrated into a right stramash, with the hapless old man at its centre.

'What? What do you mean not the same? It's Edith's will isn't it?'

'Yes, but I don't recollect this particular provision. She left the majority of her policies to – '

'Let me have a look.'

'Madam, I must protest! This is most irregular...'

'Here, let me see...'

'No, I was first...'

'Madam!'

'Sir!'

'Does this mean that Woolworth doesn't get the Jaguar? Perhaps she meant that for me – '

'Yes, after all, we are her stepchildren, you know – '

'I'm the eldest, I'm sure that it was meant for me – '

'That's absurd, Crispin. I was always her favourite – '

'Not – '

'Was – '

'Ow! Madam, you're standing on my hand.'

There was the sound of ripping paper.

'Ouch! How dare you, man, unhand me.'

A shoe flew through the air followed by a fur stole.

'Madam! Sir!'

A dishevelled Mr Crankshaw emerged from the ruck on all fours. His glasses were hanging from one ear. His hazel eyes met my nearly green but not precisely yellow ones at a distance of several inches. The old dear nearly fainted.

You could hear more sheets of paper getting torn. Little pieces showered down like snowflakes. A red wig flew out to land on old Crankshaw's head. It suited him better than it had its previous owner.

'Ah ha!'

No casual 'ah, ha!' this. This was the kind of imperious 'ah ha' that stopped an army in its tracks. The room instantly stilled, except for the Duke who was frantically searching the floor on all fours. At the back of the room I pounced upon, smothered, then ritually disembowelled the object of his search.

'This one's signed 5th October and this one, the 3rd March. Well,' crowed Aunt Maud, spelling out her triumph in semaphore code. '*This* will is clearly the one that reflects Edith's most recent wishes.'

The room subsided as people collected their wigs and dentures and counted their fingers to check that they were all still there. The ever-perceptive perfect servant, Campbell, discreetly handed the Duke a tube of Superglue.

'This is most irregular!' Overwhelmed by events, Mr Crankshaw stuck to what he knew. 'I don't remember this amended will being assigned to my keeping.'

The Gargantuan One and the Duke exchanged sly glances. The Duke had stuck the tattered remnants of his wig back on. It looked like a corbie had given him a right pecking.

'You've simply forgotten, man,' the Duke drew himself stiffly to attention, oblivious of the sniggers behind him. 'You're due to retire soon, aren't you?' he suggested unkindly, rapping the desk with his baton, making the old man start. 'I mean to say, man, you're hardly fit to hold your office. You slept all yesterday. What will Fortescue & Urquhart say? A disgrace, I call it! In my day in the army, such negligence would result in you being sh – '

'Douglas!' The Gargantuan One's look was like thunder.

But his words cowed the solicitor. You could see defeat in the set of the old gentleman's shoulders. 'V-very well, Your Grace,' he swallowed, 'as you say, a little f ~forgetful. Yes, perhaps it is time for me to retire...'

The old man meekly accepted the torn papers from Aunt Maud. He held one up in a shaking hand to the lamp on his desk. There were teeth marks. He looked through the gap towards the family. The Gargantuan One was chewing more vigorously than a Belted Galloway cow.

With a gurgle and slurp, Aunt Edith's solicitor took a sip of water and squared his stooped shoulders, as far as he was able at least.

'I shall continue where I left off...' He looked up and shrank back beneath the combined expectancy of all the onlookers. 'I leave the house and - '

'That can't be it all!' the Heron protested.

'Get a move on, man!' Crispin brushed his sister's intervention aside. 'What else has the old bask... - dear Aunt Edith specified?'

Mr Crankshaw shuddered and he could not quite conceal the distaste that congealed on his face at this unseemly funereal avarice. His mouth set in a thin white line.

'But...' Georgina hissed.

'But yourself!'

Sharp elbows dug for space.

The fixed grins were beginning to slip. Aunt Maud sat calmly, a secret smile touching her lips.

'I leave the house and estate and all its policies and paddocks to my dearest...' His helpless eyes caught Mary's and held there. The entire room was leaning forwards. Mr Crankshaw instinctively moved backwards by the same degree.

He took a deep breath. 'To my dearest sister, Maud.' Having finally got the offensive words out, he deflated, sagging into his chair like a disjointed bag of bones.

The room gasped and sat back as one. Utterly confused, the lawyer looked at Aunt Maud. He wasn't the only one. Spiteful glances bounced off the Gargantuan One's smug smile.

'What! What about me?' Outraged, Crispin was on his feet, sporran bouncing off his knees. 'I mean, what about us? We're her stepchildren.'

Unheard and unseen at the back of the room, Mary had gasped with disbelief.

Cries of distress and wailing filled the air.

'But how am I going to cope? I've just bought a new Porsche...'

'But I owe a packet at Fortnum & Masons!'

For the first time the family's tears were real. But, hollow creatures that they were, they wept only for themselves.

'No', Mary whispered. 'She loved this estate. She would never give it over into Aunt Maud's keeping. She'll sell it!'

'Hush, my darling', George soothed her. 'Hush.' Gathering her up within the cradle of his arm, he led her out. No one noticed their departure.

Dinner

Dinner was a sombre affair. Light from the brilliant chandeliers and polished silver failed to dispel the gloom.

'But she promised!' The Heron's mascara was smudged, her pretty face twisted by an ugly pout. If it rained, she'd have drowned. 'She *promised* I would get the emerald set,' she said for the dozenth time. 'They do so match my eyes, don't you think?'

'Oh, stuff your emeralds, Georgina. I'm the eldest,' Crispin complained. 'The castle and estate should be mine. The eldest has always inherited! The tradition goes right back for generations. I'm the one who has been swindled here!'

'What are you complaining about?' Nigel snapped. 'You married an heiress, after all. It's not as if you need another twenty million. I have creditors to pay.'

'Well, Maud hasn't seen the last of it,' Nigel dramatically threw his napkin on his unfinished plate. 'Oh no. I have already instructed Greyfellows & Pickering to contest the Will. I don't think the old lady was in her right mind.' He stalked out, pushing rudely past Prune who was struggling in with the champagne soufflé.

'And I have likewise instructed Rumpole & Hindsight. Step-Mama was obviously deranged,' the Heron added bitterly.

Sickened by their squabbles, Mary quietly stood up, leaving her plate of food barely touched.

'She only married him for his money,' Crispin stabbed a helpless potato.

George laid his napkin down, his appetite quite ruined.

'I don't know what he saw in her...'

Coming round the table, George took Mary by the elbow. We left them to it, bickering like buzzards over a kill. They didn't even notice we'd gone.

'We'll leave first thing in the morning,' George declared. He was disgusted. 'What a ghastly family you and your aunt had to put up with. Come on, darling, let's finish our packing and I'll get Prune to ring for a taxi. We'll catch the 10.30am train from Bridge of Orchy and I'll ring my brother and get him to pick us up at the other end.'

The weather, however, had its own plans.

116

White Out

Towards midnight, while the world slept, it started to snow. Thin and fine to start with, it brushed turrets and trees with white and tickled my whiskers, making me sneeze as I hunted mountain hare. But soon, heavy feathery flakes turned the world to cotton wool, instantly erasing my tracks as I trotted round the loch, and dampening the bark of a vixen hunting in the nearby woods. In the cold hours just before dawn the sky cleared, and a crescent moon painted the snowscape in startlingly beautiful shades of blue that radiated a soft light of their own.

In the castle, the old central heating system clanked and groaned into reluctant life, followed several hours later by the few remaining guests at Driechandubh. Mary lay snuggled against George, submerged beneath blankets and quilt. The alarm buzzed. It was silenced with a groan. Five minutes later it buzzed again.

'Right, said George, heaving the suitcases to the door. Time you were up, Mary, if we're to get the ten-thirty.'

Mary opened an eye. 'Oh, oh' she said. Wrapping herself in a dressing gown she crossed immediately to the window and threw open the curtains.

'There's not going to be a taxi and here's why.' I jumped to the sill. A familiar landscape had been stolen by winter. 'The road over the moor is bound to be closed.'

'Whoa!' George was amazed. 'It must have been snowing all night!'

Nothing was moving except a distant herd of red deer pawing through the frozen snow to get at the budding shoots beneath.

'The taxi's never going to make it through that,' Mary judged. 'There's no way. We're stuck here until the snow plough breaks through.'

Aunt Edith's Room

Breakfast was porridge and toast, and I had to find my own. None of the staff could make it from the village through the snowdrifts. Since the death of Aunt Edith, only Prune and two maids still lived in the castle, and porridge and toast was the best they collectively could do. By the time it was served, it was cold porridge and toast, which didn't do much for George and Mary's spirits. They slowly climbed the stairs back to our room

We looked to where Aunt Maud had stepped across the far landing and disappeared into Aunt Edith's room. Mary hesitated on the stairs. On the landing beside us, the grandmother clock struck nine.

'Aunt Maud! Aunt Maud!'

'It's no use, sweetheart. The old baggage can't hear you.'

'I'd better tell her we're here for another few days,' she shouted, so her husband could hear her above the racket of the hoovering maid. 'At least until the ploughs get through.'

'OK, I'll just wait for you here, sweetheart.' George wandered slowly down the stairs to re-examine the huge painting that hung facing the entrance hall. It had fascinated him since his arrival.

'Catastrophe, old chum,' he said, never taking his eyes from the painting. 'There's something about this painting that's not quite right. It's there staring me in the face but I just can't put my finger on it!'

'She's gone.'

George turned. 'What?' His head was still full of ships and sails and storms.

'She's gone,' Mary sounded puzzled.

'Well, we'll just have to tell her later.'

'No!' Mary shook her head. 'You don't understand. She didn't come out. I had my eyes on the corridor all the time. She went in and she didn't come out!'

George was amused. 'You must have just missed her, sweetheart.'

'No,' Mary was exasperated. 'No, I didn't miss her.' She lowered her voice. 'How can I miss someone that size?'

'Well, maybe there's another door?' George conceded her point.

Mary was doubtful.

'Well,' George said. 'We've got all day. Let's go and solve this little mystery.'

The room had been tidied since the burglary; it had been stripped bare.

'Aunt Maud's had it all cleared out,' Mary was miserable. 'It's all gone. The paintings…photographs…china… Everything,' she turned helplessly to her husband. 'It's as if Aunt Edith never even existed.' A tear stole down her cheek.

'But she does, sweetheart,' he wrapped her in his strong arms. 'As long as we remember her and all those wonderful memories, then she will exist.' Anger flickered on his face. No matter what that… hideous woman does. Now – '

He stepped back to take her face in his hands and knocked the suit of armour by the fire. Behind him there was the faintest of clicks and a smooth oiled sound. Stepping away, he turned his head to see what he'd done.

'George!'

'So that's her little secret. A secret doorway!'

Mary's mouth hung open, her dark eyes were as wide and round as a child's.

'There've always been lots of ghost stories about the castle, people going into rooms and not coming out. I thought it was all for the tourists! That would explain them!'

They looked at the dark doorway and back at the suit of armour. Its spiked weapon was at a strange angle. Mary tentatively cranked the mace. The wooden panel behind slid silently shut, then open once again.

'Wow!' George was impressed, his brown eyes lit with a sense of adventure.

'This is real Raiders of the Lost Ark stuff! I need my Indiana Jones hat!' He peered in, then turned back with a grin on his face. 'Let's see if we can find a torch from somewhere. May be one down stairs near the garden door?'

Mary peered in.

Follow me! I bounded ahead of them into the stale gloom. Not very high, perhaps built when men were a foot shorter, but it was wide enough, although surely just wide enough for Aunt Maud.

'Hang on, puss,' Mary called softly. 'George, where's that torch?'

The narrow arched passageway ran a short distance before the wood panelling turned to stone and the roof sloped down, so that George soon had to go forwards at a crouch. At several points the passageway branched and they opted for one or the other. Their choices finally brought us to a dead end. I sniffed the strange suit of armour inset into a niche in the thick stone. It had a familiar scent. With their inferior noses, I wasn't sure that either of my two-legged companions would detect it.

'What? What is it?' George's whisper boomed in the confined space. Head awkwardly bent, he couldn't see past her very well.

'Sshhh!' Mary put her finger to mouth. 'Put the light out,' she whispered. As darkness enfolded us, he could see past his wife to another source of light coming through vertical slits in the helm's face. 'A suit of armour' she whispered, wonderingly reaching out to touch its cold skin. She shivered. 'It's half a suit of armour, as if the back has been sliced off. It's been welded to the wall!' She peered through the visor.

'Why, it's Aunt Edith's study!'

Squeezing past his wife and stooping to look, George bent his broad shoulders and cracked his head on the capstone. 'Arrgh!' Jerking back too quickly he cracked his elbow on the corner of the passage.

He cursed. 'You go forward, darling, and take a proper look, you're smaller.'

Smaller or not, she barely squeezed into something crafted for a medieval knight. 'It's cold,' she shivered. 'Like a coffin.'

She started.

'What's happening?'

She silenced her husband with her hand to his lips and then we heard the murmur of voices ourselves. Held in George's arms with my front paws on Mary's shoulders, I watched with her.

The Duke dropped down into an armchair. 'Curse the damn snow!'

'Don't worry,' Aunt Maud smiled. 'Our unwelcome guests don't suspect a thing.'

'Still, I'll be happier when they've gone.'

'They'll be away the moment the snow clears,' the Gargantuan One crushed the other armchair into submission. 'Now we have Driechandubh and all its treasures! We've done it!' she crowed triumphantly. 'Who would have thought, when dear sister Edith fell ill two years ago, what an opportunity it would turn out to be? The money I ma-'

'We!!'

'The money *we* make from selling this midge-ridden dump will make our fortunes. We'll put the castle publicly on the market as a private sale in a week's time. After all, we still have to get over the death of dahling Edith. But I already have two bids.'

'Satisfactory?'

'Oh, indeed! The American is desperate for a castle and a title with its own coat of arms.

'And the staff?'

'Once the property is sold I'm going to sack them all. Their service to me has been less than satisfactory, as if I didn't have the right to tell them what to do.'

'Staff today,' the Duke nodded. 'Now when I was in the armed service – '

'Quite, quite,' Aunt Maud interrupted. 'Now I must get on compiling an inventory for the auctioneers. So like Edith not to have any such thing.'

'It suited us well enough when we stole her goods out from under her nose!' He followed her out of the room.

Silence.

Mary backed out of the niche. 'They've gone,' she said unnecessarily.

Aunt Edith's Letters

'What was all that about?' George pondered, after Mary had related the parts of the conversation he hadn't heard. 'What do they mean by stealing goods from under Aunt Edith's nose? It all sounds very underhand! Just what have they been up to?'

But Mary was too upset by the news that Driechandubh was to be sold and the rest of her aunt's staff were to be sacked to be of much help. However, curiosity is not just for cats, and in order to distract his wife, George persuaded her to explore further with him.

The afternoon was wearing away as the panel slid silently open. We'd spent most of our time exploring the twisting passages that riddled the thick stone walls of the old castle keep, but following my nose, I had led them through the west wing to this particular room ~ the ghastly trophy room. The shutters were closed and heavy curtains sealed the room as we stepped out into a dreadful fug. A small lamp was on in the far corner.

'Why,' Mary said with distaste, wrinkling her nose and coughing. 'It's step-Uncle Herbert's Trophy Room. How horrible! All these stuffed trophies,' she stepped in. 'But it's been occupied recently!' This time the reek of cigars and cheap perfume were unmistakable, even to them.

'Look,' George pointed towards crystal tumblers and an empty whisky bottle.

'Auchentoshan,' Mary lifted the bottle. 'Aunt Maud's favourite malt whisky!'

George frowned. 'Why pretend the west wing is unsafe when it clearly isn't? And why have a hidden room here? The castle and the east wing are huge. They could have picked any room.'

'Look...' Mary put the palm of her hand close to the grate. 'It's still warm. Why! What...what's this?'

'What?' Alarmed by his wife's silence, George knelt down beside her.

'Mary', he asked softly, 'what is it? What's wrong?'

Hand shaking, Mary picked up a half-burnt piece of envelope with the tongs. Carefully holding the smouldering remnant, she brushed away the burnt flakes and spread what was left on the hearth. George still didn't understand why she was so upset. His knees cracked as he knelt down beside her, a frown on his handsome face.

'T-this is Aunt Edith's writing. L-look at the envelope, George!' she was quite overcome. 'Look! It's addressed to me!' Mary held up the partial address for him to examine. 'Dated... 18 January.' She tried to pull the letter out but it was too badly damaged.   And look, the fireplace is full of letters. She did write to me, George, Aunt Edith did write many times!' She raked amongst the ashes trying to rescue more fragments, but it was hopeless; they had gone on the fire first. 'Why on earth did her own sister burn them?'

George carefully peeled away the remnants of a diary out of the charred cover and opened it out. The delicate paper flaked at his touch. 'You can still make some of this out,' he said frowning.

'*Still confined to bed. Exhausted. Doctor Fraser remains baffled by my condition*', George read. '*He cannot account for the continuing headaches, stomach cramps and poor vision. He would like to move me to hospital in Inverness for more tests, but Maud insists he continue to treat me here. She says it is for the best...*

He shook her head. 'I can't make out any more of this page.'

Taking the fire tongs, Mary pulled out the smouldering remnants of several other pages.

'*McFie,*' she read, '*has discovered a number of...miss...*must be *missing paintings and antiques. When I challenged Maud on her return, she said that they had been sent to Mosswood & Dunwoody in*

123

Edinburgh for cleaning and restoration. She said they were sent on my very own instructions! She maintains that the stroke has left me confused and forgetful, but that is quite untrue. I rang Mosswood & Dunwoody. They have received no commission on my behalf in over a year. Maud is lying. What is she up to?'

'Here, sweetheart, take a look at this one!' George turned the torch so that he could read better in the poor light. 'The first half is illegible but you can just make out the second page.'

'A nurse sent by Doctor Fraser has been attending me in person for the last week, supervising my routine. I feel greatly improved and was able to venture out of my bedroom today for the first time in months. I unexpectedly came across the Duke in Herbert's study. He has no business in the west wing. He claims he was lost, but I do not believe him. The room stinks of the man's cigars. I suspect that he and Maud are up to no good. I have told McFie that the Duke is no longer welcome at Driechandubh. Now that I am feeling slightly stronger, I am going to tell Maud she may leave as well. I have left her in charge far too long.*

*I will write to Mary again. I don't understand why she has not visited for so long. I have a suspicion…the rest is burnt.'

George paused to pick out another half-burnt fragment. 'Here's a date, sweetheart! August 20th Not long before she died. Listen to this!

'I have discovered their secret!' Puzzled they looked at each other. 'They have been… the next part is smudged. I can only make out theft and treasure. But wait! The third page is ok: I have told Maud I have discovered what she and the Duke are up to. They are behind all the thefts in Braeside and they have been hiding their stolen goods down in the cellars here at Driechandubh! She claims no one will believe me. She says she has been telling everyone for months that the stroke has left me muddled. They will all think my claim is nothing more than a figment of an old lady's imagination. I fear for my life -'* George frowned and shook his head. 'No. I can barely read the rest.'

'I fear for my life?' Mary looked at George with horror. 'What does she mean? They wouldn't! They couldn't have!'

George was already examining more pages. 'Look at the handwriting, Mary!'

Mary gasped as her husband held the burnt diary up for his wife to see. The unsteady scrawl that rambled across the page like a drunken spider was blotched and smudged. He read out the small portion that didn't fall into ash.

'Dreadful headaches...Tried to get up but collapsed... forced me back to bed. Dizzy and nauseous. I fear Maud is preventing McFie from entering my apartments, and I am too weak to rise from my bed. She says it is for my own good, and that I am too ill to receive visitors. But where is Doctor Fraser? I keep asking Maud to send for him...Then there are empty pages till here...

Have been unable to write in my journal, as I have been so dreadfully sick...

Every time I begin to recover I fall ill again, and each time is worse than the last. I think I am being poisoned! I am so weak I can hardly stand unassisted. I... Why has Mary not come?

'Right,' George's mouth was a grim line. 'We'll take these as evidence. Deliberately withholding medical care; that's as good as murder. That should be more than enough to get that harridan locked up for a long time!' Carefully he held the smouldering diary.

What's that?' Reaching for the poker with shaking hands, Mary lifted a log and gently eased out a thick sheaf of papers barely singed at the edges. They bent eagerly over their latest find with childish curiosity.

'What are they?'

'Hang on,' George said. 'Let me get some light.' They shuffled over to the pool of yellow beneath the table lamp. 'It's a Will! It's your Aunt Edith's Will! The Will dated 3rd March. They've burnt her Will? What a strange thing to do!'

'Isn't it, though?' George was becoming suspicious. He thumbed through the flaking pages. 'To... to...to...here we are! To my dearest sister, who cared so tenderly for me in my illness, I leave my heartfelt thanks, as she already has taken possession of much of my jewellery and several valuable paintings.'

'My - my heartfelt thanks!?' But that's not what Mr Crankshaw said!'

'No it wasn't, was it? Mary!' George voiced a suspicion. 'Is it possible your Aunt switched Wills? Would Aunt Edith really leave everything to a sister she didn't even like? After asking her to leave Driechandubh?' He was still speed-reading, rapidly turning from page to page. 'That would explain the solicitor's confusion!

'To...blah' he skimmed the pages. ' To...what!!' He read it again.

'What is it? You've gone white as a sheet!'

'I-I,' he croaked. 'I leave the house and estate and all its policies and paddocks to my dearest niece, Mary, who is the daughter I never had!'

'What?' It was the merest whisper. They looked at each other with eyes that were round as the full moon. 'According to this, you've inherited Driechandubh! The other will must be a forgery. I wonder...' George's eyes narrowed. 'I wonder if that 'accident' at the start of our stay was really an accident?'

'George!' Mary was shocked. 'Surely they wouldn't have tried to kill us!' Mary still believed the best in everyone.

He shook his head. He was a better judge of people. 'I'm not so sure, Mary. Anyone who can ruthlessly isolate and manipulate a confused and dying old lady to keep her from the one person she really loved, in order to swindle the inheritance...well, I'm not so sure.'

It was too much for Mary.

'Hush, sweetheart, hush,' George tried to quieten her anguished sobs. He rolled up the remains of the will and pulled out his mobile. 'No reception. Damn! Must be the blizzard. I think we'd better get out of here and call the Inspector as soon as we can.'

Wiping her tears away, Mary knelt by the fire hearth. 'Let me get some more of these letters first. It's all I have left of her.'

How I wished I could cry out. I mewed but they were too distracted. I felt her coming, heralded by a huge displacement of air,

126

by the floorboards vibrating beneath her heavy tread. But someone with a much softer tread arrived ahead of her.

With a cat's sixth sense for survival I slunk beneath the dresser and watched as a pair of polished court shoes appeared round the door. Mary and George were too intent on the evidence of greed and treachery that littered the room. Too intent on comforting each other to hear the slight creak of a floorboard out in the hall; too intent to notice as the darkly clothed Duke softly took a shotgun from the wall and loaded two cartridges into the breech. To give him credit, he could move as silently and lightly as a cat inside a house. The metallic click as he deliberately closed the breach made them turn to confront the twin barrels of a shotgun aimed at them. It was already too late. Cruelty and coldness had entered the room, already calculating how to turn the situation to her advantage. Oozing malice from every pore, Aunt Maud slid up behind her accomplice.

'Such a great pity for you, don't you think,' Aunt Maud smiled cruelly, 'that it snowed?'

Cambridge and Cat Burglars

'So...' Her pale blue eyes flicked from Mary to George and down to Mary's hands, where she clutched a handful of Aunt Edith's letters and George held a still smoking Will. 'You have discovered some of our little secrets have you?' Her gloating face was beaded with nervous sweat. 'I'm surprised, my dear, that it took you so long. Given that you grew up here, I was so sure you must have known about the hidden passageways and priest holes. Many old castles have them, you know. People always have secrets to hide.'

'So it's true,' George said flatly. 'Mary has inherited Driechandubh, not you! That Will read yesterday was a fake. You let your sister die just so you could get your hands on her money!' He was disgusted. 'How could you? That's tantamount to murder.'

The Gargantuan One smiled unpleasantly. 'I dooo so like life's little luxuries, and her London house in Bishop's Avenue is so expensive to run, yet Edith always was the one to have the luck. And she found out that we had been selling one or two Rembrandts...the odd piece of jewellery.'

'So it was *you*,' George accused. 'Not the storm! You did try to kill us with that gargoyle!' He stepped forwards threateningly. 'You harridan! I'll- '

'Oh no, you don't,' the Duke dipped the barrels of his shotgun towards Mary. 'Don't try anything silly or the girl gets it.'

George turned back to his wife. She was white as a sheet in the dimly lit room. He took her hand.

'But you,' Mary looked at the Duke with disbelief. 'But you have Cranbruik Estate,' she was baffled. 'You have so much already. What more could you want?'

The Duke smiled thinly. 'Alas no, my dear, there is no longer any fortune to go along with the estate, only debts. Some of my ancestors chose the wrong side in the 1745 Jacobite Rising and things have been going downhill ever since. And I have a certain lifestyle to maintain.'

'A playboy,' George provoked the Duke as he helped his wife to a chair. 'Gambling.'

'Gambling,' the Duke agreed. 'A gentleman has to have a fitting pastime. I have an image to maintain for the public, until I find a suitable heiress.'

'So you took to petty theft as a cat burglar?' George was trying to goad him into a fight.

'Yes,' the Duke smirked, tweaking his waxed moustache, 'and a very accomplished one, if I do say so myself. It was so easy, like taking candy from a babe. To begin with, at Cambridge University, we'd do it for a lark. All those high society dinners and parties…all that jewellery draped around creamy necks and empty heads. Being heir to a dukedom opened every door. They queued up to choose me as an escort. Everyone assumes you're a rich playboy; playboy, yes, but sadly not so rich. Grandfather and father squandered most of the remaining family fortune, and I had an unfortunate dabble with the stock market.

'And… one thing led to another. A couple of racehorses…a yacht…a house or two. My cars – vintage Aston Martins and my McLaren F1.' He sighed theatrically and raised his eyebrows with a casual shrug. 'The more I stole, the more I spent; and the more I spent, the more I seemed to need. You know how it is?'

'No,' George said contemptuously. 'We don't. We spend only what we earn.'

'And that,' smiled the Duke, 'is not very much, is it? I for one like more excitement in my life. And things were getting a wee bit tight financially. I had to sell the horses, creditors were closing in. Edith's stroke couldn't have come at a better time. Driechandubh was ripe for the picking.'

'A painting here… an antique there…' Aunt Maud took up the story with relish. 'Edith was too ill to notice what we were up to. But then, we thought, why not Driechandubh itself? Six million in the bag! It was so very easy to tell everyone that her health was steadily deteriorating. And if she suspected we were stealing from her, who would listen? After all, people often become confused after a stroke.'

The Duke nodded. 'Using the secret passageways, it was easy to overhear her and her lawyer drafting the Will and easier to steal it away and forge a copy. I am an adept forger if I say so myself!'

'By the time that prying butler of hers discovered the thefts,' Aunt Maud was enjoying herself. 'It was already far too late for both of them. She was already dying. We just had to finish her off a little earlier than we intended. Digitalis in her herbal tea, you see. Edith's favourite flower! Foxglove has all the same symptoms as a heart attack. No one suspected a thing. Not even the doctor.'

There was a stunned silence. Unmoved by Mary's tears, Aunt Maud took a poker to the fire, rousing the bricks of peat from their rosy slumber into fiery hunger. She held out a doughy hand weighted with Aunt Edith's jewellery.

'Those letters, my dear. Yes, those pieces you're clutching. We'll make sure they all burn this time.'

We watched, as one by one, she fed them into the fire. The fears and ramblings of an ill and confused lady who was slowly being poisoned by her own sister went up in smoke. The Will followed.

Such a Tragic Accident

The silence was brittle with fear.

'What are you going to do with us?'

Aunt Maud smiled at her niece. 'Why dahling, you are going to have a tragic accident.'

'And just how are you going to do that?' George challenged, inserting himself between his wife and Aunt Maud. 'Not the easiest thing to do, given there's the two of us. Another two deaths will be suspicious, don't you think?'

'Really?' Aunt Maud's red lipstick stretched. 'Do you think so?' she added softly, malice dripping like melting ice. 'No, there you are wrong. In the Highlands it's the easiest thing, isn't it, my dear?' She turned to George's wife, watching her closely.

Mary gasped. She knew what was coming.

'Why, you read of it in the papers all the time,' Aunt Maud waved the fire poker in the air. 'Stupid careless people who wander up the mountains without proper clothing or equipment as if they were out for a stroll in Hyde Park. Hypothermia sets in so very quickly and minor accidents rapidly become fatal. And there is always the danger of avalanches isn't there, my dear?'

Mary gasped, spots of high colour burning her pale cheeks.

'Why, y – '

'Get back,' the Duke raised the gun barrels threateningly at George's chest, forcing him back beside his wife.

'Have you seen the forecast?' the Gargantuan One licked her lips with relish. 'No? What a pity. Radio Scotland have issued blizzard warnings across the Highlands and the temperature will drop to minus six degrees in a matter of hours, but of course, being young and foolish you will ignore the warnings,' Aunt Maud paused to smile at Mary. 'Just like your stupid parents did.'

Mary swayed against her husband, but her eyes blazed hot with anger.

'The mountains look so romantic covered in snow, don't you think?' Aunt Maud continued. 'We'll drop you off somewhere so far from anywhere you won't know which way to turn. By the time we call out the Mountain Rescue in the late evening, it will of course be too late. At minus six you'll not last two hours. No, my dears, no one will suspect a thing. Just another tragic accident,' she put hand to bosom in mock grief. 'Losing one so young is always a great pity, but of course, as everyone knows, you were always such a delicate creature. And,' her eyes narrowed. 'Too close to Edith. Close enough to uncover our little enterprise. Now,' she said, suddenly abrupt. 'We've brought your jackets, hats and gloves,' she kicked a pile of garments forwards. 'You would at least have that inadequate protection outdoors no matter how foolish you were, don't you think?'

She turned to the Duke.

'Give me the gun. Take the Land Rover in the garage, Douglas; it's fitted with snow chains. And bring it round to the old west wing door. That way Prune or those dozy girls won't see us. Make sure you find some rope to tie their hands.'

He nodded and was gone.

'Time,' she smiled, 'for a little adventure.'

She herded them outside through the darkened corridors of the deserted west wing to where the jeep waited. Trembling with fear, I shadowed them, keeping well out the way of the shotgun.

'Right,' Aunt Maud said with a grim smile of satisfaction, as the Duke tightened the last knot around Mary's wrists and checked George's ropes a second time. 'In you get, the two of you. And take that flea-bitten fur-ball with you. I'll stay behind, Douglas.' Slamming the rear door, she handed the shotgun to the Duke. 'That way I can cover our tracks. Make sure the alarm isn't raised until it's too late!'

A Little Adventure

'I know where w-we are,' Mary said defiantly, clutching me for warmth and protection, knowing perfectly well that the Duke would shoot me just for the pleasure of it. 'I know these roads. We're out on Dramossie M-moor.' Jaw clenched, she was already stuttering with tension and cold. 'H-h...heading for the Kelpies Cliffs.'

'Why, yes, you are correct, my dear,' the Duke wrenched the wheel to one side. Turning off the main track on to an old drover's road the jeep bounced and careened off tussocks of grass hidden by deep snow, throwing George hard into the metal grille that separated the driver from the back seats. Unable to move his bound hands quickly enough to save himself, George crumpled to the floor with a moan.

'But...' the Duke continued without a pause as we bounced around. 'That knowledge does you no good. The satnav, as you can see, knows nothing of this old road and you're three miles from anywhere as the crow flies. You – ' He fought to control the wheel as the jeep lurched violently through a deep snowdrift. 'Have nowhere to go out here. You'll never make it back to the castle.'

The windscreen wipers could barely keep up as the snow fell thicker and faster. The Duke cranked the hand brake. Snow touched to butter by the headlights swirled in and out of view in the bright white darkness. Yanking the steering wheel to the left, the Duke turned the jeep round and round in circles so that no one was sure any longer which direction we had come from and I felt sick to the pit of my stomach. Leaping out, he opened the rear door and the blizzard reached in with cold grasping fingers.

Farewell!

'Yes,' he shouted. 'I think this spot will do very well, what? What? With the snow gates closed on the moor, no one is going to come this way for a long time. Come on,' he gestured with his gun. 'And the mountain rescue shall of course be sent on a wild goose chase in the other direction.'

Cramped limbs and captive hands made his captives awkward. The wind was edged in steel and already cutting through their inadequate clothing. Blood had congealed on George's head. Dizzy and disorientated, he stumbled to his knees.

'Farewell!' The Duke bowed mockingly before leaping into the front seat. Small satisfaction that just before the door closed, a flash of russet caught the light before being taken by the storm. May his bald head freeze! Cloaked in snow, the jeep was swallowed by the blizzard in moments; the dark spongy juices of the bog soaking up its tyre tracks, the white darkness soaking up the headlights.

Caught by the ferocious wind, head down against the driving snow, Mary blundered against her husband who was groggily trying to rise. Wind whipped her long hair around her head and into her eyes. With a sudden cry of despair, she realised a contact lens was gone.

Beneath their combined weight, the frosty crust of the bog cracked and broke. Deep, dark peaty water welled up into her house shoes, and a small heel snagged in heather throwing her forwards. I pressed my furry warmth against her. Roused by her plight, George groggily fumbled with tied hands for the penknife the Duke had thrown from the window as a parting gift, but in the faintly luminescent dark he misjudged the spot. Frantic minutes passed as he sank frozen hands into the freezing water again and again before he found the small knife. Awkwardly he opened the blade and sawed down on the rope round Mary's wrists. By the time she cut his ropes they were already soaked to the skin and shivering uncontrollably. George had lost all feeling in his hands and blood was spilling from shallow knife cuts as well as from his head.

'We h-h-have to find sh-sh-shelter!' The wind whipped his words away. 'Or we're going t-to die! Hold onto me, whatever happens we mustn't become separated.'

'Aunt E-e-e-dith said t-t-there are caves... I-I-in the headlands. At-a-at Kelpies Cliff. She t-t-told me stories about smugglers...smugglers who used old p- passageways between the caves...a-and the castle. B-but there was a terrible cave-in one stormy autumn o-over a c-century ag-go. Aunt Edith-h said the caves are dangerous now, so we never went near them.'

George hesitated to turn away from possible rescue, but a slim chance was better than no chance at all. 'Dangerous or not, they can't be as dangerous as staying up here on the moor! We'll die of-f-f hypothermia here. We have to find them!'

'Which way? Which way?'

Panic tinged their words. They no longer knew which way they faced in this white world, but I could smell the sea and I could feel and hear its thunder and boom vibrating beneath the storm. I darted forwards then raced back; repeatedly darted forwards then raced back.

'Catastroph-ph-phe will find shelter! Animals have great instincts for survival,' George cried. 'Sweetheart, hang on to me and follow Catastrophe!'

Stumbling blindly, they turned and followed me into the teeth of the storm and away from Driechandubh.

I danced from boulder to boulder but the bog sucked at their feet, treacherous heather roots tripped them time and time again. Reeling drunkenly from exhaustion and soaked to the bone, they made pitifully slow progress. Then Mary lost first one shoe then the other, lacerating her feet on crusted ice. After that, George had to carry her.

Wet flakes of snow thickly coated hair and eyelash and coats, and the high wind made breathing difficult. Mary and George were becoming invisible. So was I! I took to circling around them so that they could still see me. The ground became firmer underfoot as we reached the edge of the moors, but by now George was also stumbling and falling from exhaustion and pain. Tripping, he fell to his knees, the force of it punching the breath out of his lungs and tumbling Mary heavily onto the ground. Neither of them got up.

The wind shifted. Huge snow-capped boulders loomed into existence scant feet away and the boom of the sea was loud. If there were caves, they were here. High above, through ragged gaps in the cloud, white stars appeared though lacy clouds. The snow lessened and the night turned bitter. Wrapped warmly in my fur coat, the cold couldn't touch me, but if George and Mary didn't move soon, they would die.

I rasped George's cheek with my tongue anxiously mewling. Finally I nipped his ear hard. That stung enough to get his attention.

'Shelter!' George shook his wife but got little reaction. Crawling to his feet, he moved ahead to examine the gaps between the boulders in the hope of finding some meagre shelter there, but he was far heavier on his feet than I was. With barely a shout he fell through the snow crust and disappeared, as if the mountain had devoured him whole. It seemed impossible that such a big man could be swallowed by such a small gash in the ground. I pawed at Mary.

135

'George!' The wind took her full-throated cry and tore it to shreds.

Kelpies Cliff

'George! George!'

Roused to sudden action by finding herself alone, Mary was frantic, screaming, crying and digging at the frozen snow with bloodless fingers, tearing them raw and bloody on gorse and ice. She was trembling violently, her breath coming in ragged gasps.

'Mary!' The cry was faint, too faint for her ears to hear.

Trusting to my instincts, I followed George's voice and dropped through the hole in the ground. Mary screamed, but I yowled even louder as she tore a hank out of my tail in her effort to save me. I heard her cry of despair as I, too, was swallowed by the earth.

Caution and pain unsheathed my claws, which was just as well. Sixteen well-honed crampons barely slowed my backward fall. The slope wasn't too steep, but the stone was weathered smooth by centuries of wind and rain that had frozen into a solid waterfall. In a shower of frozen dirt and ice I dropped on top of George, winding us both. He hugged me to him before peering up the shaft towards the faintest patch of moonlight.

'Mary!' He threw everything into it but she couldn't hear him over the wail of the wind.

George could not climb back up. The drop from frozen shaft to cave floor was too great and the ice too sheer. Mary would have to come down and George knew it.

'I think... I must have...' George fumbled with unfeeling fingers in his pockets. 'I knew it!' he cried, striking the lighter he waved its feeble glow from side to side. 'She must see it surely?' he muttered anxiously.

For a moment he seemed at a loss but then began a second search of pockets.

Turning up a pencil and Aunt Edith's half-burnt diary, he tore off the corner of an envelope and wrote two wobbly words. He then tucked the piece of paper under my collar.

'Right, puss. Up you go!' Using all of his remaining strength, he hurled me as far up the icy shaft as he could. The first time I gained no purchase and landed back on his head, further injuring him. Twice more I scrabbled for purchase, leaving deep scores in the ice before he simply raised me to the chute and waited until I had found purchase. Slowly I pulled myself up, paw by paw.

It wasn't easy, and my injured leg muscles were burning as I breasted the lip of the shaft. The snow had completely stopped and a thick silence had fallen on the deserted moorland. The temperature was also dropping like a stone. To the east a rising three-quarter moon threw pale light on the snowscape.

Huddled in the lee of the boulders, Mary was almost unconscious. I licked her face and nuzzled at her with increasing urgency. Finally I bit her hand. I had to draw blood before she roused herself enough to understand I was back, but her speech was slurred and confused.

'C-c-c-c-catastrophe? Whash i-s-ssh it, boy? Where ish he? Where ish h-h- he?' The scrap of paper rustled against her face. With shaking hands she pulled it out and peered at the two words scrawled in a child's wobbling hand: Trust Catastrophe.

'Mary!' her husband's voice boomed up the ice chimney. 'I'm all right. Mary, you've got to follow Catastrophe! Here boy. Here puss.' Reluctantly I dropped down the icy shaft a second time. George was better prepared and gathered me up and deposited me on the floor of the hollow. 'Mary,' he bawled, looking up too late. 'You've got to let go. Trust us! Trus-oooffhhh!!'

With a thin shriek she cannoned into George, knocking them both to the hard packed floor of the cave. The lighter flew out of his hand and went out. Bones splintered. In the dark George heard his wife moan.

'Mary? Mary? Are you alright?' Cursing George blindly fumbled around searching for his lighter. Cats' eyes are six times better than two-legs'. Darting forwards, I mewled and led him to it. Its wan light revealed the brittle ivory bones of countless small creatures that had cushioned Mary's fall from the chimney. It also revealed lacerated burns on her bare feet and legs where the rough ice had scraped the skin raw. It should have been painful but she appeared not to notice. It was clear she could no longer feel her hands or feet.

'G-g-george?' she sat up with his help, blinking owlishly in the pool of light. 'Wh-w-what'-t-t? Wh-where are we?'

'Hush, sweetheart, hush,' he hugged Mary to him. 'I'm all right. We're all right! I think we might have found a way down to your Aunt Edith's caves.' He held the light up for her to see by, but she shivered and jerked in sudden fits and starts and found it hard to concentrate on what her husband was saying.

It appeared as if a natural rift had been chiselled into the cliff to create a vast stairway, a seam into the dark heart of the earth. It was clearly man-made and perhaps that is what helped George come to a decision.

'Well...' he sucked in a lungful of cold dry air and let it out thoughtfully. 'We're out of the c-cold now. But how w-w-will anyone find us down here? How will they even know where to look?' he swallowed and closed his eyes. 'The Mountain Rescue could walk within feet of the ice flume and not know we're down here.'

'Right,' he grunted as he lifted his wife. 'We can't get back up,' he kept talking to her even though she made no response. 'Let's see if we can find a way down to the sea-caves. Then you and Catastrophe can stay there and I can go for help along the beach once the tide's out.'

I forged ahead, constantly turning back on my tracks to guide them. No stray starlight found its way into this subterranean world, so I trusted to my other senses to chart our path through the endless blackness. Currents of air flowed around me, revealing hidden paths and dead ends. Fresh air and sea air eddied and mingled. Fissures and tunnels ran off in random directions, but I always chose the downward sloping passages. My own movements sent out tiny ripples that returned to describe cave walls and passageways and boulders. Each and every breath echoed softly or loudly or not at all, hinting at a low ceiling or some vaster cavern.

Halfway down to the sea, George stopped to rummage in his jean's pockets. Tearing at the waxed paper he made his wife take the toffees. 'Chew this, Mary. Sugar ~ to give you energy.' Even that small effort was almost beyond her.

Some paths were of no use and I had to turn back. They were dead ends blocked by massive rock falls, or simply too narrow or too short for George and Mary to squeeze through. Slowly, by trial and error, I navigated our way downward to the sea caves they hoped lay at the base of the cliffs. At last my paw dipped into lacy pools of seaweed and salt that sucked and swelled with the hidden tide. Behind me, I heard a stumble and a cry. Mary had fallen badly. It temporarily roused her

'I shink m-m-my ankle's sprained. Y-y-ou've got...got... you've...' A fit of shivering took her. 'Y-y-you've got to leave me.' She was brave and stubborn, making him both proud and fearful at the same time. He shook his head and kissed her.

'I can hear the s-sea. We must b-be close to the cliff face. I'm...I'm going to search for a way out, anything that might help us attract attention. Here,' he took his ripped jacket off and sat her down on it. He pulled his mittens over her bruised waxen feet.

'I won't go far, sweetheart,' he tried to reassure her. 'I'll just take a quick look. Hold on to Catastrophe, he'll help to keep you warm!'

She nodded wordlessly, holding me to her chest where I lavished her with furry warmth and affection.

The huge limestone cavern we were in was faintly illuminated by the sea. It glittered with a soft diffused phosphorescence that entered in through undersea tunnels that opened out to the rocky shoreline. There was a curse as George tripped, followed by a triumphant shout.

'Wood... Mary, I've f-f-found driftwood! And it's dry! We can start a fire. Mary? Mary?'

Hastily he gathered up a clumsy armful, all the while calling.

'M-mary? Mary?'

But she made no response as I curled on her lap. She was shivering, her breath slow and shallow as she fell unconscious. George had no experience, but he instinctively knew she was in serious trouble. The tidal wave of fear that rocked him as he knelt beside her was not for himself, but for his wife. He touched the back of his trembling hand to her chalk white face.

'Hypothermia! Oh, dear God, let her b-be alright. F-fire. Must g-get a fire going.' He held up his lighter and shook it. 'Not much lighter fuel left,' he muttered anxiously.

He stood for a moment debating over what to do next. Thrusting hands into his pockets he pulled out a crumple of half burnt paper; evidence of dire deeds at Driechandubh. He looked down at me as I curled around Mary.

'N-not-t much use, Catastrophe, if we die h-here.'

He took off his heavy wool jumper. Then he thrust the diary back into his pocket and held the lighter to the rest. His frozen fingers were so clumsy he could barely hold the lighter, let alone coax a flame. But after a frustrating few moments a tiny wisp of smoke curled upwards. Hands now shaking violently George let the fire take hold before holding it to his jumper. The oily yarn burst into flame. Holding his breath, George laid a few pieces of driftwood across it and then more. The dry wood sparked and cracked and smoked... and took! Foraging by its dancing yellow light, George gathered up more wood until he had a bonfire chasing back the shadows. He made his wife as comfortable as he could, then agonised over what to do next, talking all the time to me.

'If I stay, help might arrive t-too late. If-f-f I leave, she might die down here alone and afraid.' He shook his head. He could no more leave her than his own heart. But I could. I left him cradling her in his arms, a silent waterfall of tears streaking down his dirty face.

The cliffs were riddled with combs and shafts but there was one passage in particular, almost hidden by a huge rock-fall that attracted my attention. I slipped between boulders and stones. Beneath the dust and rubble I could see the chiselled outline of steps. The air was stale and heavy, but the tiniest thread of fresh air ran through it. If Aunt Edith's story of smuggler's caves were true, I hoped this passageway would lead back to the caves beneath Driechandubh.

The Mountain Rescue

A helicopter clattered overhead as I emerged from the caves beneath the castle, sending me into a frenzied panic for cover. The machine landed on the lower gardens whipping the snowdrifts into a storm while I cowered down beneath some bushes.

The lights on top of two jeeps turned urgently, belting the castle and loch in their icy blue beams. Big bearded men who moved lightly on their feet, quietly checked equipment and stowed it inside. More were arriving on skis, their bright red and yellow jackets moving in and out of the light. Radios chattered like magpies. One rescue team was already out on the moors to the west. I had heard their muffled shouts and the barking of dogs as I padded beneath their feet along the narrow tunnels hat fanned out like veins, deep beneath the moor.

Slowly, keeping to the shadows, I edged closer to the castle where a familiar voice boomed out in the still air.

'You must hurry,' said Aunt Maud, clinging to a wiry, fox-faced man with a white beard and a hooked nose, who was trying to load a jeep, only every time he moved she appeared to accidentally get in the way.

'My goodness, do be careful with that ice axe, young man!' she cried loudly in a youngster's ear, causing him to drop rucksack, ropes and axes down the stone steps with fright.

The tough, grey-haired man, trapped against the stone wall by Aunt Maud's bovine bulk, rolled his eyes in terror. I'd wager he'd have rather faced an avalanche. Having caused enough chaos and consternation, she moved inside to see what damage she could do there. I followed.

'Oh dear, I'm just distraught!' Aunt Maud cried in the entrance hall, which was nothing compared to the distress of the man who leapt up with a scream as somehow or other Aunt Maud managed to spill half a dozen mugs of hot coffee over his unmentionables. What he said was also unmentionable.

'Where's Ian?' the Team Leader asked, turning from his conversation by the fire. 'Hasn't he found those maps yet?'

I had spotted a man in the Map Room, attempting to peel off Aunt Maud who was sticking to him with the tenacity of a plaster.

'I'll take three of the chaps towards the White Corries,' the Duke suggested loudly as he strode in. 'Mary was talking about taking up skiing again.' He had a dark woollen hat pulled firmly down over his bald head.

The Team Leader shook his head at the folly. 'In this weather? I thought she was an experienced skier?'

There was a crash and a curse from the Map Room and the sound of tearing paper.

'Will *someone*,' the Team Leader said through gritted teeth, 'get that wretched woman out of the way? We're already delayed by half an hour and more snow's on the way.'

'The RAF helicopter's here,' a voice called from outside.

'Has the doctor arrived yet?'

The man on the steps shook his head. 'Any minute now. The police helicopter is bringing him in. ETA ten minutes.'

I slipped unnoticed between feet in stout boots and gaiters, and headed down to the kitchens. I didn't fancy my chances if the Duke or Aunt Maud saw me first.

Cook was in her favourite chair by the range, sobbing into her apron. Two bearded, red-haired giants were trying to comfort her. I dare say she wasn't a woman often given to tears.

'Don't you be fretting so. We'll find them, Ma, won't we, Willie?'

'Aye, that we will, Ma. Me and Dougal's going - '

Willie looked up.

'Stone the crows! It's a wildcat! And what a state he - '

'It's Himself!' Darting forwards, Cook scooped me up. She was strong for such a small woman. She must have been, to raise sons like these.

'It's Catastrophe! Mary's cat. Why he's filthy and his fur's frozen!' She clumsily wrapped me up in her warmth. 'Judith, lass,' she turned to one of the maids. 'Stop your snivelling and get some milk warmed.' As Cook set me down on her lap, blood seeped through her apron. With a cry of alarm she held me up. 'He's injured, and chust look at the state of his poor wee paws. The wee fechter must have walked miles! He was always with Mary. She's out there somewhere! She's in trouble isn't she, laddie?' she asked me.

A huge hand cradled my paw, examining the chalky bloodless pads, the ragged claws. 'Early stages of frostbite, Ma. He'll need treated.'

To tell the truth, I could no longer feel them. They were torn and bloody from ice and rock and frozen bog, and from that long climb up the icy shaft.

'What's that?' Cook caught a hint of something falling to the slate slabs in a pool of melting ice. The big red-bearded man scooped the broken sprig with his huge hand and gave it to his mother. Bending down he ran his hand along my pelt picking out several other sprigs.

'Why,' Cook exclaimed. 'That's roseroot, and this is wintergreen. They're very rare hereabouts. They're only found together at Kelpies Cliffs. You know where she is, don't you, Catastrophe?'

Braeside CID

The remaining volunteers were crowded round a huge map laid out on the dining room table. A heated debate was taking place.

'I'm not willing to commit all the remaining volunteers in one direction on the basis that the wildcat knows where they are. We already have a police team out to the west on the lower slopes of the Five Wizards. How long have they been missing?' the Team Leader looked up at the Duke.

He appeared to consider the question. 'Can't be more than two hours,' he lied.

The Team Leader nodded. 'They can't have reached Kelpies Cliffs on foot in under three or four hours, Dougal. Not in this snow.'

But Dougal was determined. 'Ma says Mary and this chap are inseparable. She says to go to Kelpies Cliffs.'

That made them listen. Cook was obviously held in high regard.

'That's absurd,' the Duke was scathing. 'It's just a mangy wild animal. How could it possibly know where they are?'

'Because,' Dougal repeated. 'Ma says they are inseparable. And because of these stuck in the ice of his coat.' Dougal held up the two sprigs. 'Roseroot and wintergreen. Ma knows her plants. This combination's only found on the Kelpies Cliffs.'

The Team Leader nodded. He looked round the table. 'That's good enough for me. Take the police chopper the moment it and the Doc arrives.'

'But,' the Duke protested. 'This is absurd. What happens if they're to the south? Surely you'll allow me to take a team to the Corries?'

The Team Leader thought about it. 'Right, John...Richard... Sean. You three stay with His Grace in reserve for just now. But everyone else to Kelpies Cliffs, stat. I'll wait till you call in, before I dispatch a team to the Corries.'

'I'd like to come,' a voice cut across the bustle and clamour. Heads turned to where a red-haired footman was putting down a tray of hot drinks.

'And who are you?'

'Campbell McFie.'

'Well, Campbell, thanks all the same, but we don't take civilians with us on S&R.'

'I'm not a civilian,' the young man held up a wallet. 'Braeside Police CID, and before that the Black Watch. I grew up here. My grandfather was Findlay McFie, butler to the Lady Edith. He taught me my hill craft.'

'Good grief! But you've grown, lad! Well in that case, you're doubly welcome. We're struggling. Half the volunteers have been unable to get through the snowdrifts on the moor.'

'I'll get my kit.' Campbell was gone.

But he'd tipped his hand. Hand on her bosom, Aunt Maud had turned white as a sheet as she sifted through the implications. Both a policeman and the grandson of the butler she sacked! One coincidence too many. Mean eyes flicked from side to side as if expecting arrest at that very moment, but the volunteers were dispersing to their tasks, leaving her and the Duke alone by the coffee table. They didn't dare touch me, so they ignored me. The Gargantuan One lit a cigar with trembling hands, took a deep drag and coughed till her eyes watered.

'Calm down, Maud!' the Duke hissed, his moustache quivering. 'There's nothing to worry about. They can't have survived this long, what? What? It's over three hours since I left them, and the temperature out there is minus eleven and still dropping.'

'But what about Edith? The police must know we murdered her! Why else plant a spy in the household?'

'Nonsense!' the Duke rolled his eyes. 'If the police even suspected we murdered your sister, we would have been arrested long before now, what? What? No. At the very worst they must have suspicions about our little thefts. They – ' The pair fell silent as

145

Campbell and Dougal emerged from Below Stairs, rucksacks and ice axes slung over their shoulders, talking about equipment.

'Just keep your nerve,' the Duke hissed out of the side of his mouth, keeping his voice low. 'And we're sitting pretty. Driechandubh is ours now. Even if we are convicted of theft, no one can take that away from us. It would be worth a few years in jail. '

'There you are!' Striding into the entrance hall, Cook's second son, Willie, effortlessly scooped me up from beneath the table and raised me onto his broad shoulders. 'Dougal! Campbell!' he called. 'That's the police chopper arrived. Wish us luck,' he said, turning to the Duke and the Gargantuan One. 'Don't worry,' he added, seeing their horrified expressions. 'We'll find them! Catastrophe here is going to show us the way!'

The Ice Chimney

Below us, the police were beating across the moor, strung out like bobbing lanterns, while the dogs ran to and fro. We left them far behind. Snow skirled, whipped to uncanny patterns by our passage. Caught in the searchlight, a herd of red deer fled before us. So this is the freedom of the feathered folk?

The ground hurtled by below.

Ice.

Snow.

Rock.

Wind.

This was my world.

I struggled frantically in Campbell's arms, anxious to be down.

'Put us down here, Jock. Catastrophe knows where to go.'

The rotors slowed. Whump,...whump... whump... whump... Rescue One put down on the flat cliff top. Whump...whump...

Opening the door, they watched as I cast around for scent and track. Shouts and torches and crunching ice told me they were following. I danced forwards.

'That cairn!' Nimblest on his feet, Campbell arrived first. The frozen cusp of the hole barely held his weight as he crunched over to peer among the snow-capped boulders.

'Wait!' the youth shouted, palm raised. 'The ground's treacherous.' He might have been young, but Campbell carried himself with a new confidence now that he had shed his guise as a footman. Dougal and Willie moved up to join him. Behind them, the helicopter engine was killed and the remaining volunteers jumped out and started to unload their equipment.

'Look!' Willie pointed to where I danced. 'Blood! And the ground looks unstable around the lip. They must have fallen through here.' Testing the ground with ice axes, the volunteers circled the black gash in the snow. Seven torches searched downwards into the gloom.

'It's an ice chimney! Smooth as a flume. About a forty five-degree angle,' Willie judged. 'Crampons and ropes, lads. We're going underground.'

'I'll go first,' Dougal took charge. 'Then Campbell, you bring the cat down so he can lead us. Willie, Jock, you have experience of pot holing and caving, so you're next. Doc...wait here till you get our call. If they fell down they'll likely have injuries, and we'll need to get you down by the quickest route possible. Right lads, set up base camp here.'

I watched with interest as a rescuer belayed out the rope anchored to a boulder. Dougal abseiled swiftly down into the maw of the cliff. Like a cat, his crampons and ice-axes gripped the folded sheets of ice, lending him claws to descend safely.

'About thirty feet down,' he radioed up.

Quickly knotting a rope, Campbell clipped the karabiner to his climbing harness already weighted down with pitons and pegs. Ice axes in each hand, with me in a rucksack strapped to his chest,

Campbell began the climb down. The moment his feet touched the foot of the ice pitch he released the ropes and put me down.

Dougal and Campbell's helmet-mounted torches examined the chamber. 'In some kind of passageway,' Dougal talked quietly into his radio as two more volunteers descended. 'We're on the right track; lots of frozen dirt and gorse here on a bed of old broken bones. One or both of them fell down. There's traces of fresh blood. We're following the cat…Doc, down you come.'

They were mostly big men, the Mountain Rescue. And like George, the volunteers found parts of the route a tight squeeze as they negotiated the maze of damp boulder-strewn tunnels that burrowed down to the sea.

'Looks like that tunnel's blocked by a rock fall…Stairs? There are stairs disappearing down into the cliff…the passageway's branching, take the right fork…looks like they passed this way. There's some toffee papers… still following the cat…damn! We've lost him!… No, he's back! I can see the bottom now, where it levels off, got to be near to sea level by now…nearly there…a cave! Big one…

Another cave…no it's a huge limestone cavern…stalactites…it's like a cathedral down here…there's been a major cave-in at some point…more boulders…a fire!'

'Fire?!' the radio crackled into life.

'Aye, I can see a fire…just…climbing over…boulders…huge cavern…fire…dying down…I can see them…I can see them! Get the Doc down here, ASAP.'

We found them next to the dying fire, their skin chalky and sunk as cold candle wax.

'We have them! We have them!'

'Roger that, Willie. Doc's on his way down. Advise condition.'

'George…head injuries…only in his tee-shirt! Semiconscious…violent shivering…shallow breathing…weak pulse. Mary…unconscious…erratic pulse. Severe hypothermia. Looks like she sprained her ankle. We have to get them out of here!'

They were already pulling equipment from their rucksacks. 'We're wrapping them in foil blankets to conserve body heat.'

'Roger that, Willie. Doc's just behind you.'

George's eyes flickered open. He opened his mouth and tried to sit up.

'George,' the Doctor had arrived, followed by two stretcher-bearers. Thickly wrapped in blankets and insulating foil, Mary was getting gently lifted and strapped onto one of the stretchers.

'George, rest easy, we've got you both. We're going to airlift you to hospital. Here drink this,' the Doc held a thermos of hot coffee to George's bloodless lips.

George almost choked as the hot liquid coursed down him, but his eyes opened and focused on the men in front of him

'M-m-murder,' the single croaked word brought Campbell instantly to his side. The policeman fumbled for his police badge and held it up for George to see.

'Braeside CID.'

George's eyes widened. 'Mur...der...' He held up a fist closed tightly around a half burnt diary. 'Aunt Maud,' he whispered, thrusting the papers into Campbell's hand. 'Murder!'

As the Mountain Rescue began the laborious trek back to the surface, with Mary and George on stretchers, Campbell hastily read the damaged diary George had given him. The young policeman raised his radio and spoke to the helicopter pilot waiting for them out on the moor.

'Patch me through to Inspector Morrell immediately,' he demanded. 'And call in Rescue Two.'

The Cat's Out of the Bag

Thunk...thunk...thunk...thunk.

The police helicopter, Rescue One, ate up the miles to the castle. Rescue command at Driechandubh had been informed that George and Mary had been found alive, but that their condition was critical and they were both unconscious. The net was finally closing around Aunt Maud and the Duke, but the Inspector did not want to flush out his prey until his men were in place to make an arrest. He was gambling on their avarice and greed, hoping that would keep the pair of them at Driechandubh if they thought there was still a chance they had got away with murder. RAF Rescue Two was racing George and Mary to the hospital. Campbell had gone with them. The police rescue team had been hastily recalled back from the moor and the Inspector was making his way through the snowdrifts to the castle.

We arrived first. Willie carried me up to the house wrapped in a huge blanket, my paws now salved and bandaged. Eyes bright from tears, Cook rushed out to take me into the entrance hall. Willie wrapped the two of us in a huge hug as anxious volunteers crowded round, keen to hear first-hand about the rescue.

'They're both alive! Catastrophe found them! They're suffering from acute hypothermia but the doc's already treating them.'

'Oh!' Aunt Maud's smile was stretched tighter than her corsets. Her face was pasty white. 'Oh, how marvellous!' But warning bells were beginning to ring.

'How are they?' Striding over from the Map Room, the Duke's voice barely wobbled, but I could smell the physical stench of fear that radiated out from him.

'Were they able to say anything?'

'George was sinking in and out of consciousness.' In his elation, Willie had forgotten the Inspector's instructions. 'Totally delirious… They're in safe hands now. That's the main thing!'

The Duke swallowed.

'It was a near thing, though!' Willie plumped me onto his mother's lap.

'Mary was lapsing into severe hypothermia. Pray God we reached them in time!'

'So he'll...they'll recover?' Aunt Maud's anxiety was unfeigned, though for all the wrong reasons.

'God willing!' Willie reassured her.

'Where's Campbell?' Her sharp eyes missed nothing.

Willie frowned. 'He went with them on Rescue Two. He'd found some papers clutched in George's hand that he seemed to think were pretty important.'

The Gargantuan One's eyes widened with shock but no one was watching her.

All eyes were on Willie.

'You were right all along, Ma, you and Catastrophe! They'd fallen down an ice chimney that led down into underground caves,' he pointed to the map on the table. 'Here! The cliffs are riddled like a comb with sea caves and passageways. I never knew they even existed.'

'Mistress Edith did,' Cook nodded. 'She must have told Mary. But why would they be out there in this weather, so far from home?'

'There was driftwood. That's what kept them alive. One of them managed to get a fire going. That's what saved them in the end. That and Catastrophe. We'd have never found them in time without this chap!' He leant forward to tickle me under the chin.

In the midst of their quiet optimism, sharp blue eyes sought out the Duke's. They hadn't planned for this. They'd been so sure George and Mary would be dead long before the Mountain Rescue reached them. So sure they had got away with murder. The Duke bobbed his head slightly. He knew the cat was finally out of the bag, and it was only a matter of time before the police came for them. Driechandubh was lost.

'Well, that's jolly good news, what, what? Great team effort. Well, must get the Land Rover into gear, what what? I take it you'll want to get to Inverness Hospital as soon as possible, Maud? To see your niece?' He added, meaningfully, as the Gargantuan One stared at him blankly.

'Why, yes. Yes, of course. My dearest niece.' Aunt Maud nodded. 'What a relief she's still alive. I'm quite overcome. I'll just fetch my coat. Yes...my coat.' Turning she headed upstairs.

The Gargantuan One should have followed the Duke immediately, but greed and habit won out over common sense. Almost spitting with suppressed emotion, she was outraged to have lost at the last hurdle. Her newly found wealth, her high society friends were now lost to her forever. All her wicked plans had come to nothing. Well, she was not going to leave empty handed!

I followed her upstairs where she strung pearls and diamonds about her neck and emptied gold and gems into her coat pockets. Hoisting her petticoats the Gargantuan One filled her bloomers. The remainder from a half dozen jewellery boxes was swept into an enormous handbag.

Gravity and Gold

Blue, red and white lights were racing up the drive. The Inspector was minutes away. Aunt Maud reached the top of the garden steps and came face to face with exhausted police volunteers coming in off the frozen moors.

'I must get to my niece's side!'

Aided by gravity and gold, the grief stricken Aunt Maud was an unstoppable force. Coins and jewellery spilled into the snow from bulging pockets and hidden petticoats. She mowed volunteers down by the dozen as she went one way and they the other. Equipment and people spilled down the steps.

The police lights were stationary, headlights half buried in a snowdrift. Figures were wading through the snow.

'Stop them!' The Inspector's faint cry was lost amongst the cries of anger and anguish, as the Gargantuan One trod on bodies in her haste to get away.

'Where have you been? Get in, get in!' the Duke hissed, his voice strung high with fear.

'Quick, man,' the suspension dipped as Aunt Maud hauled her bulk through the door. 'The snow will hide us!' The Duke gunned the accelerator. The lights of the jeep swung in a crazy arc, belting shades of blue with gold as he threw the jeep into overdrive. Loud voices called from the driveway. Inspector Morrell was on their heels.

'Stop them! Stop them!' But in the stramash, nobody yet understood what he meant.

The jeep lurched backwards, slamming into the jeep behind. Its glass windscreen shattered. Changing gear, the jeep leapt forwards, knocking a car out of the way with a screech of protesting metal and ice. The Duke's own precious, pillar-box red McLaren F1!

Dramossy Moor

'Arres…Arrest them!'

Breathless, hatless and pipeless, the winded Inspector had finally arrived, his breath billowing and sparkling around him as the bellows of his chest rose and fell. He was too late.

The Duke smiled as he revved the engine. The snow chains bit, showering the Inspector with dirty ice. With scant inches to spare, the Inspector dived to one side for his life. Gathering my hindquarters, I leapt from rucksack to bonnet to the Land Rover's roof rack as the jeep gathered pace. I nearly fell. A cat with bandaged paws cannot grip with its claws. The Inspector was shouting for the police helicopter. The hunt was on!

The jeep hurtled down the paddock track, heading for Dramossy Moor. The east wind had freshened and was driving snow and the conspirators before it. Powdery snow skirled round the Land Rover and floated in through the open windows. Gears clashed and grated as the engine attempted a superhuman feat. Behind me, I heard the by now familiar rhythmic growl of engines, as the police helicopter took to the skies.

Thunk…thunk…thunk… thunk… A searchlight swept the darkness.

Jolted and jarred, the Land Rover bounced me around cruelly. The snow was falling faster now. If it got any thicker it would hide them and ground the helicopter. The Duke had put the headlights out and was driving blind, trusting to memory. He changed down a gear and put his foot down. But the jeep could run no faster. It cracked off a boulder. On the left hand side the snow chains snapped. Aunt Maud shrieked.

'The lights, man! Put the headlights back on. You'll kill us!'

Got You, You Odious Creature!

The jolting and cracking ice was fearsome now, as the wounded jeep lurched from lochan to lochan, so he put his lights on again. Snow fell thickly from all directions at once. Icy water gushed and the hot engine growled. Steam rose in great glittering clouds from under the bonnet, as the Land Rover climbed out of the water.

They were doubtless surprised at the strength of the sucking bog, how its dark juices pulled the jeep to its heart like a jealous lover, refusing to let go, clinging to the very last. Alas for Aunt Maud, the Land Rover's suspension was quite worn out. It had spent all afternoon cavorting across the ice-clogged moors. The Gargantuan One was the last straw.

The helicopter's searchlight was sweeping the moor behind us. The noose was tightening. The jeep was bouncing recklessly over whale-backed boulders when catastrophe struck. Too late, they saw the huge, smooth-surfaced lochan, glittering deep blue in the headlights.

Aunt Maud screamed.

The freezing crust fractured, followed by the jeep's suspension. With a screech of tearing metal and splintering ice, it sagged and subsided into the bog. The peat soaked water belched loudly as the jeep started to sink. The Duke cursed.

In front!

Behind!

The hunt was closing!

The beaters were flushing their prey.

The Duke leapt out into the deep chest high water. Struggling for high ground, he vanished into the dark. Let's see how far he can flee before the icy night takes him, or the police catch up with him. How does it feel, Duke, to be hunted down like one of your trophies? A pity they wouldn't stuff him and mount his head on the wall when they catch him.

There was a crack and a scream as the weary jeep door gave way to gravity and deposited Aunt Maud into the bog. She tried to cry out as the dark juices oozed up around her, smothering gold's bright gleam with tawdry mud. The bog belched and burped and made satisfyingly unpleasant gurgling noises.

They were both in my world now.

Our eyes met.

Got you, you odious creature!

Glossary of Scottish Words

Awfy ~ (pronounced aw-fi) Means awful

Bagpipe ~ A musical instrument. A set of pipes (chanter and drones) and a bag held under the player's arm

Bannock ~ (pronounced ban-nok) an oatcake

Beastie ~ Any small animal or insect including spiders and creepy-crawlies but widely used for larger animals

Blaeberry ~ (pronounced blay-ber-ree) Edible purple-black berry

Blether ~ (pronounced bleTH-er) To talk or chatter, or a conversation or chat. A very talkative person can also be called a blether

Bodhran ~ Traditional drum struck with one hand using two-headed stick

Bonny ~ Attractive, beautiful

Bogles ~ A ghost

Burn ~ A brook or stream

Cairn ~ A pile of stones

Cairngorms ~ A smoky quartz originally found in the Cairngorm Mountains

Canny ~ Astute or cautious

Capercaillie ~ (pronounced cap-er-kale-yee) Large woodland grouse

Chitter ~ To shake with cold. To shiver

Carfuffle ~ A disturbance, commotion or disorder

Cock-a-leekie ~ Soup made from a fowl and leeks

Corbie ~ (pronounced korb-ee) A crow or a raven

Corrie ~ Circular hollow on a hillside

Courie ~ To nestle or snuggle down

Croft ~ A small enclosed plot of land with a cottage

Cullen skink ~ Fish soup made from smoked haddock and milk

Crabbit ~ In a bad temper or grumpy

Dinnae ~ Do not or does not

Dram ~ A drink of whisky

Dreich ~ (pronounced dreeCH) Wet dismal weather

Eejit ~ Idiot

Fash ~ Means to trouble or bother

Fechter ~ Fighter

Fend ~ Struggle or strive to get by

Foosty ~ Mouldy

Footer ~ To potter or fiddle around

Forebye ~ (pronounced for-by) Means besides or in addition

Ghillie ~ (pronounced gill-ee) guide for fishing or shooting

Glaikit ~ (pronounced glay-kit) silly, foolish or thoughtless

Gloaming ~ The period of twilight at dusk

Himself or Herself ~ The most important person in the household

Keek ~ To peep or glance at something

Keen ~ To lament the dead

Kelpie ~ In Scottish folklore a water spirit in the form of a horse that lures travellers to their deaths

Kippers ~ Herring that is split, dressed, salted and smoked

Kirk ~ A kirk is a Presbyterian church

Lad(die) ~ (rhymes with daddie) A boy or a young man

Laird ~ A lord who owns a large estate

Lament ~ A slow traditional song or pipe tune composed for a death

Lass(ie) ~ A girl or young woman

Loch ~ A lake

Lochan ~ A small loch or lake

Mince ~ Grated meat cooked with onions and dumplings

Muckle ~ Something which is muckle is large

Neuk ~ (pronounced nyook) A nook or corner

Polis ~ (pronounced po-liss) The police

Porridge ~ A dish made from oatmeal cooked in water or milk

Postie ~ Postman or postwoman

Quaich ~ (pronounced kwayCH) shallow drinking cup

Reek ~ Reek is to give off smoke / to smell

Rowan ~ Scottish name for the mountain ash tree

Sleekit ~ Superficially charming but actually untrustworthy and sly

Stane ~ A stane is a stone.

Skelf ~ A splinter, particularly one embedded in someone's skin

Skirl ~ A loud shrill sound used to describe bagpipes

Sporran ~ Pouch, traditionally fur, now faux fur which hangs from belt in front of kilt

Stovies ~ A traditional dish of sliced potatoes and onion cooked in dripping

Tapsalteerie ~ (pronounced tap-sl-tea-ree) Upside down or untidy and chaotic

Tattie-bogle ~ (pronounced tat-ee boh-gl) Scarecrow

Trews ~ Close fitting trousers generally part of a uniform

Wabbit ~ Tired and run down.

Wee sensation ~ A small drink of whisky.

Whisky ~ An alcoholic spirit produced by fermenting cereals, particularly malted barley.

17759318R00087

Printed in Great Britain
by Amazon